For Wesley

Love & Laughter
Alyne Bailey

Red Helmet On A Motorcycle

Alyne Bailey

Publisher's Note:

This is a work of fiction. All names, characters, places, and events are the work of the author's imagination.

Any resemblance to real persons, places, or events is coincidental.

Solstice Publishing - http://www.solsticeempire.com/

For the man who introduced me to riding motorcycles, who encouraged me to get my own bike, who has supported me every step of the way, and who has proven he is a keeper even after all of these years, my husband, Harry.

Chapter One

All I need to do is sign the papers, and the Goldwing motorcycle will belong to someone else. How can that be hard? It is just a signature, and I've done that a million times in my life. This signature doesn't even need to be notarized. Signing means the motorcycle will no longer belong to me, and I move on with my life. I can't even ride the bike. It's a really big, heavy motorcycle for a woman. My husband Jim died over a year ago and had been so sick for weeks before that. We never got to make that long cross-country trip. We had spent so much time planning it as we argued about freeways and back roads. Jim would want someone else to have the chance to make such a trip. The decision to sell the bike seemed like a good idea two weeks ago, but now it is suddenly so painful. I really thought I had progressed past this. Everyone at Hinshaw's Honda has been so kind. They helped me get the bike from our house to the store and quickly found a buyer. All I need to do is sign this last set of papers, and it will be done.

"Mrs. King, would you like me to get you a cup of coffee?"

"Thanks, Brian. It might be just what I need, and please call me Maggie."

"Take your time. I'll be back in a few minutes."

Brian is such a nice young man. *Oh my goodness, I sound like my mother. When did I get so old that a man in his early thirties was a 'nice young man?' If I'm not careful, I'll turn into a little old lady before I hit sixty. I guess I could be worse. He is tall, slim, and has a cute curl in his hair that falls on his forehead. I always have the urge to push it out of his eyes. Does that make me a cougar?* I had best turn my thoughts back to the papers sitting in front of me. Brian has been very helpful throughout this whole sale process. He specializes in bike consignments. I am sure most of his sellers can't wait to get their money. Staring at the papers isn't going to change anything. I am a fifty-five-year-old widow with two grown children, a house in Federal Way, Washington, and a good job as an escrow agent. It is time to let Jim go, and for me to really start my life over again. Everyone tells me that I am strong and that I can do this. So, I'll paste a smile on my face and sign the documents. The smile does not fill the hole in my heart. *Oh, Jim, I miss you so much.* I turn to see Brian walking back toward me with a cup of coffee in his hand.

"Here is the coffee I promised, Mrs. King. I didn't ask how you like it, but I have creamer and sugar packs in my pocket."

"Black is just fine, Brian. I've signed the papers. What happens next?" I hope I have managed to keep my voice level. Please, no tears now.

"It will take about fifteen minutes to finish with the buyers and have the office draw your check. You can sit here with your coffee, or you are welcome to wander the store. I can find you when I'm done. Who knows? Maybe you will find a bike for yourself. We've got some great ones."

I watch Brian say a few words to a couple standing beside our old bike as he walks to the office. I assume they are the buyers. They look excited, and I am happy for them. I remember how excited Jim had been when we bought the bike. It was to start a new chapter in our lives. Now I'll be starting that new chapter all by myself.

At 5'5", I know I could never handle eight hundred fifty pounds of motorcycle like our Goldwing. That was Jim's dream bike for the two of us. He said it was a Cadillac of a motorcycle complete with cruise control, an intercom system so we could talk as we went down the road, and even heat to the footboards for those cool mornings. We made one overnight trip before he got sick. Eight weeks later he was gone, and with him all of our hopes, dreams, and plans for the future. I've picked up some of the pieces of my life, but this bike was the last part of Jim. Time to make some changes, and if I sit here one more minute, I'll be in tears. Jim would not have wanted that. Time to wander the store.

Hinshaw's Honda is a large motorcycle store located in south King County displaying both new and used motorcycles as well as a small selection of riding gear. We had purchased our bike here. In the front windows, they have a row of big bikes just like our Goldwing in an array of colors and ages. Big bikes are designed for highway cruising. They can accommodate two riders comfortably, and often appeal to older couples.

The middle section has small bikes, some quad runners, and a few dirt bikes as well as a number of desks for the sales people. Along one wall is a display of smaller, sleek bikes called "crotch rockets" by most bikers. That type of bike is usually purchased by mid-twenty to thirty-year-old men. The bikes are fast, and the rider must lean forward over the gas tank. A number of motorcycle companies produce that style. As I walk up to a row of the crotch rockets, I'm surprised to see a group of men both young and older discussing the bikes. *Why would a row of crotch rockets draw a crowd?*

"What in the hell are those things?" asked an older gentleman.

"They are scooters," replied one of the younger ones.

"Nah, scooters look like the old Vespa from when I was a teen."

"You mean they actually had bikes way back then, Old Man?"

"Snot-nosed kid. You're right, though. These must be scooters. You can get on it without throwing your leg over the gas tank. Where is the gas tank?"

"Well, it must be under the seat although that one is open and has room for a helmet or two there."

"From the front, all of these bikes look alike with the difference just increasing motor and tire size."

"Someone was smart arranging them this way. Scooters beside a similar-sized crotch rocket. They got my attention. Not that I would ever buy one."

"Well, I could see where it might work with the arthritis in my hip."

"Sure thing, old man, that would work for you. Or for a woman."

As I move from in front of the bikes to the side of the row, I can see the alternating pattern. I had never noticed scooters that looked like these. I also had thought in terms of an old Vespa when they mentioned scooters. These look like actual street bikes. A glance at the speedometer on one of them shows it goes to one hundred-twenty miles per hour. The tag on the largest reads Bergman 650, and another is a Bergman 400. "I bet I could ride one of these." *Oh, did I say that out loud?*

Out of the corner of my eye, I can see a tall man looking at the row of bikes. His longish hair hangs below an old do-rag matching his scraggly beard and old worn leathers. Mirrored sunglasses cover his eyes. My first impression is a dirty, crusty old biker straight out of a Marlon Brando movie. I can barely hear him as he mutters, "Ride one if you want, but those are not bikes." He turns and heads toward the door. I watch him walk away. He looks much too rough around the edges to be a Honda rider. I have guessed right, when I see him walk to his Harley Road King. He fires it up, and roars out of the parking lot. The men from the scooter discussion watch him go with smiles on their faces. Does every man really want a Harley? The whole scenario makes me laugh.

"Great laugh, Lady. If you came with one of those scooters, I'd buy one."

I have to laugh again, "Afraid not but good try." It feels really good to laugh at something a man has said. I can't remember when I have laughed twice at anything. Things really are changing.

"Mrs. King, here is your check, although it sounds like you should stick around and help me sell some of these bikes.

"Thank you, Brian, but I'll leave the bike selling to you."

"Take care of yourself and call me anytime if I can be of assistance."

"I may just do that. Thank you again."

Today has been a good day after all.

The two people I had seen earlier beside our old bike are now in the parking lot wearing our old helmets and settling on to the Goldwing. I wonder where they will go on their first long ride? It is time for me to head to Kent.

Chapter Two

Going for an evening walk with my girlfriends is always a good way to clear my head. Our favorite walks are those on the Green River Trail in Kent, a small slice of nature in a suburb of Seattle. Kent is also close to where all of us work and live. We are free to discuss our jobs, lives, and issues. Over the years, they have provided me with laughter and allowed me tears. We have had many discussions about selling the Goldwing. They have understood how difficult it has been. Tonight, I'll buy the wine after our walk as we celebrate that accomplishment. I am very lucky to have such good friends in my life.

Claire Murphy is over fifty, but refuses to discuss her age. She likes to keep her hair freshly colored to hide any gray. She is married to a truck driver who criticizes everything she says or does. None of us know why she stays with him, but we will always listen when she needs to vent. She is a mortgage loan officer in an office adjacent to mine, so we have lunch often. We've been friends for almost ten years. She always finds new adventures for the four of us to share.

Megan Jones works for a publishing company and flies all over the country, although, she often talks about settling down in one place. We are all jealous of her travels. She leaves her dog, Muffin, with me when she is on the road and tries to join us whenever she is in town. Her belief in metaphysics adds a calming effect to the group. She is the oldest at fifty-seven and isn't afraid to let her gray hair show but often spices it up with a fun color. She likes being single and thinks all single women should use a dating website. She dropped lots of hints but always tried to be subtle in suggesting I try things.

Denise Stockton is the youngest at forty and is a single mom raising a son she adopted. She got married and divorced in a six-month span a few years ago. She now vows she will remain single forever. As an instructor at the local community college, she is the most conservative of the group. We often manage to shock her with the things we say and do. She likes to tell us that she walks with us, so she knows what not to do in her own life. She is our counterbalance and the first to put us into a fit of laughter.

"Did you really sell the motorcycle?" Claire asks, tossing her hair over her shoulder. "Did you see any cute single Goldwing owners while you were at Hinshaw's? You know that they have to have money to afford that type of bike."

"Yes, I sold the motorcycle, and no, I didn't notice any single men riding Goldwings. I don't think I'm ready to be a back seat on another Goldwing right now no matter what."

Megan chimes in about the salesman Brian. "I'm sure that he was not just nice to you because it was his job. Many younger men find mature women attractive. Your silver hair is more platinum blonde and vibrant rather than the dull gray like mine."

"I will repeat that Brian is not interested in me. In addition, he rides a crotch rocket. There is no way I'd ever get on the back of one of those!"

"You are all wrong. The best motorcycle men ride Harleys, and you are not mature. All three of you are just plain old," Denise adds with a giggle.

"There was a Harley rider there, but he was so grubby. I actually think he smelled bad; he was disgusting. In my defense, I may not be as old as you think because I did see a scooter that might be just my size."

"Oh yeah. Proving my point that you are old by wanting to ride a Vespa!"

We can't keep the giggles from erupting. "This was more crotch rocket than Vespa. It has 650 cc's with an automatic transmission and a step through design, so I don't need to be six feet tall to put my feet down. It is really cute and looks fast. I could do my own riding rather than being a back seat."

"Go for it, girl!" Megan exclaims. "I think all women should plan to ride their own bikes rather than just being a back seat. The back seat can be a fun option when you want to wrap your arms around a man and press your breasts into his back to let him know you are there. Riding your own bike means you can be in control of your own life. It will also remind him to treat you with respect. Tough decision."

"I'm not considering a bike to earn respect from men."

"Do we get to help you pick it out? I think your bike should be red," Denise adds. "Red is such a hot color. Considering how old you are, you will need all the help you can get."

"You'll need new riding gear. We can all go to Destination Harley in Tacoma. I'm sure they have the best gear and there will be loads of Harley men there. We could help you pick out one!" Megan tugs on my sleeve as she raises her eyebrows in Groucho Marks style.

With that kind of support, I think it may be time to do more research on scooters. I might even go back to talk to Brian. It would be best to not take my friends with me. Their behavior would be too much like kids in a candy store; only they would be shopping for men on motorcycles. I may not need a man, but I really liked the feeling of freedom that came from riding with Jim. I'll bet I'd feel the same way on my own bike. For now, however, it is time to steer the conversation away from bikes as we end our walk and agree on a location for our celebratory glass of wine.

As I drive home, I find myself considering what buying a bike might mean. What will my children say if I buy a large scooter? At twenty-two and just out of college, my son, Richard, would love to have a Harley. He had teased his dad about riding an "old man" bike when Jim bought the Goldwing. Will he think I'm now having the midlife crisis? He has said I needed to find myself, but is riding a motorcycle too much at my age? Maybe I just need to join a book club or something tamer than a bike. My daughter, Sharon, is more conservative than Richard. As they grew up, she liked playing the big sister trying to keep Richard in line. She is now all about being the proper wife and mother. She is a good mother, and I'm sure a good wife. I swear she focused more on an MRS. degree in college than an actual degree for a career. She was ecstatic when Thomas asked her to marry him. She feels she has the perfect life being married to a banker. Will she be shocked if I make this purchase? She did try to convince Jim that riding the Goldwing cross-country was a bad idea. I'll never hear the end of it if I tell her I'm planning a cross-country trip. I can't see myself doing that, but I'm not too old to try something new. I guess it is my duty to make my son just a little jealous and to shock my daughter.

I'm ready for some fun in my life, and this might just be the way to do it. Maybe Denise is right. Red might be a good color for my big girl scooter.

Chapter Three

When my children were toddlers, I loved taking them to the mall. I didn't do a lot of shopping, but it was a wonderful place to let them stretch their legs on a rainy day. We would look at the window displays, and they would tell me stories about what they saw. The mall would often be decorated for holidays or have special displays down the center such as cars or RVs. I find myself smiling, remembering their excited chatter.

Of course, by the time they were teenagers, their chatter was not so exciting. Richard absolutely hated shopping for new school clothes. We had even tried to have Jim take him shopping. Jim wasn't that fond of the mall himself, but he did try with Richard. They would come home with one pair of jeans and a T-shirt. Once I knew that those items fit, I could return to the store to buy another set. At least he didn't object to my selections. Getting him into clean clothes was a problem until he reached seventeen and discovered girls. Shopping is still not one of his favorite activities.

Sharon loved to shop but hated having me along. We didn't always agree on what was appropriate for her age. She preferred to join her girlfriends on those trips. She thought I really should have just handed her my credit card. Selecting a prom dress was a nightmare. When it was time for her to head off to college, she became much more conservative about her clothing. She announced that she didn't want to attract hordes of boys but only a man of purpose. I had to work hard to have her include a party dress in her wardrobe. Shopping for it was still not a fun time. I had been surprised when she asked me to join her when she shopped for her wedding dress.

My friends and I enjoy catching the train down to Portland for a day of shopping for professional clothes. Portland has many of the same stores that are in Seattle or our surrounding malls, but it is just more fun to take the light rail over to Lloyd's Center or to the boutiques in the downtown area. By taking the train, we are able to enjoy a glass of wine or margarita with lunch before we need to drive home. Shopping should be all about relaxing and having fun. Sometimes we act more like teenage girls with our giggling than our actual age.

Once the children were more independent, Jim and I started enjoying antiquing weekends. He would select a new place to go, and I'd find a Bed and Breakfast for the weekend escape. It was never about whether we found something to buy or not. We had fun in our search. It also gave us time to simply spend quality time together. Now it is hard to look at those treasures without remembering the good times. Looking at them puts such an ache in my heart. When it came time to shop for his dream bike, I left it all up to Jim. He could discuss engine size and speed without me standing there trying to pretend I was interested. Once he had made his decision, I joined him when we selected a color. Of course, I agreed with what he wanted. Isn't that why it was his dream bike?

Throughout this last year, I have hated shopping. It had been so hard to make all of the decisions for Jim's funeral. Neither of us had wanted to believe his death could be that quick. He had wanted to discuss the possibility, but I had resisted. I didn't want him to know how scared I was. He knew anyway. After he died, I found the letter he had written to me. He shared his desire for a simple memorial service and a green burial in Ferndale, Washington. I followed his request, but it still involved making so many decisions about his green casket, flowers, music, and location for the memorial service. The children and my friends were there to help me, but I hated every minute of it. Each selection seemed to take Jim further away from me.

Now, here I am considering shopping for a motorcycle. I wish I could just go online and pick out one. What will the sales people be like? Will they talk down to me like the men who tried to sell me my laptop? I knew what I wanted and did not need their 'help', but all of them thought they needed to mansplain it to me. I'm not sure I can handle that as I start shopping for the right bike for me. I will need help understanding my options, but I don't need to be treated like 'the little woman who is unable to make a decision.' I wonder how many sales women I'll find. Will they be any better, or will they also talk down to me because I'm an older woman? Should I go after work when I'm professionally dressed or only on Saturdays when I can wear jeans and boots? Am I sure I want to do this?

I finally decide to go on Saturday morning. I still have to push myself out the door reminding myself that I can do this. I have dressed in my best jeans and boots, although not motorcycle boots. I really don't know if I will be riding on bikes or just sitting on them. If I decide to look at motorcycles rather than just scooters, I'll need to be able to swing my leg over the seat. Jim used to say he was glad he was tall as he did that. Am I out of my mind to even think about this?

Last night, I had checked my options for motorcycle dealers in the Seattle area. Today I'll start with the Seattle Scooter Center. They have scooters from 49 cc to 500. I am fairly certain that I want one that I can ride on the highway. I won't be able to do that with 49 cc. From the Scooter Center, I will continue on to make a loop including the Triumph, BMW, and Ducati dealers.

Taking a deep breath, I slide out of my car and step through the door of the motorcycle shop. The showroom is a maze of bikes of all styles, sizes, and colors. A very young man greets me with a smile. "Good morning, how can I help you?"

"I am thinking about buying a scooter."

"Well, you've come to the right place. Let's start over here with our Havana Classic series from Lance. It tops out at thirty miles per hour and comes in an array of feminine colors. We also have similar models from Kymco and Sym. For any of these, you do not need a special license to ride them. Also, we can get cargo trunks to match your bike. What color do you like?"

Oh my god, I really have reached the little old lady on a Vespa stage of my life. Do I really want to continue with this? "To be honest, I am looking more toward a highway bike than just something to putt along on. What do you have in the 400 to 500 cc models?"

I thought he was going to start sputtering before he shut his mouth and then says, "Well, let's head over this way. Will you be the one riding this bike?"

"Yes, I will. My husband and I had a Goldwing for the two of us. He passed away, and I think I'm ready to ride on my own." *Gee, I can say that out loud.* Is this step one, or is it step two because just coming in the door seemed like a big step?

Things go much better with the BMW, Triumph, and Ducati dealers. I want to believe that I am more confident in knowing what I want. I am now able to discuss engine sizes and gears on both scooters and motorcycles. I sit on a dozen different models of scooters and look closely at the small motorcycles. My head is spinning with prices and specifications. A glass of wine with a veggie stir-fry for dinner may be just what I need. I'll put my feet up and relax with a movie.

I've saved Hindshaw Honda for Sunday. I called yesterday to confirm that Brian will be working. He doesn't specialize in scooters, but I felt comfortable working with him. If I do buy from them, I'd like to know that he gets the commission. Now, I just have to hope that he doesn't give me the little old lady approach.

Chapter Four

It is so much easier to walk into Hindshaw Honda on Sunday morning than it had the day I completed the sale of the Goldwing. I move to where Brian is sitting at his desk. "Good morning, Brian. I was hoping you would be here."

Brian looks confused, "Good morning, Mrs. King. Is there a problem with the sale of your Goldwing?"

I smile as I take a seat at his desk and say "Oh no," shaking my head. "Nothing like that. I am actually thinking about taking your advice. I think I want to get a bike to ride myself. I looked at a number of models yesterday, and I'm now here to see what you might suggest."

"That is great. So, let's start with the basics. What kind of riding do you want to do? Short trips around town or longer rides on the freeways or something in between?"

'Right now I can't see myself on a long cross-country ride, but I know I want enough power to ride with freeway speeds, but still light enough that I can handle stop and go traffic in the city. I remember how challenging that was for my husband with both of us on the Goldwing."

"Well we have motorcycles and scooters that might do the job for you. Why don't I ask Christine to join us? Height and weight are more important than you would think. At 250 pounds and 5'11" my needs for a bike are not the same as yours." Brian turns toward a woman sitting at a nearby desk. "Christine, can you join us as Mrs. King looks for a bike for herself?"

Standing, Christine walks over, extending her hand, "Of course. Hi, Mrs. King, I'm Christine Stone. So you are thinking about riding. Are you looking for a new or a used bike?"

Christine looks to be about my height and probably fifty years old. She wears her blonde hair in a long braid over her shoulder and looks comfortable in her tucked in white shirt, jeans and boots. Her smile lights up her whole face.

"Nice to meet you, Christine. I haven't decided for sure, but my instincts are toward a new bike. I know that Honda has changed their lineup of large scooters, but that is as far as I've gotten. And please, call me Maggie."

"Maggie it will be. Let's start over here at our display for scooters and smaller bikes. I'm assuming that you are not looking for a dirt bike, but I really hate making assumptions."

I laugh, "You've made a fair assumption."

Brian adds, "And she is looking for a highway bike rather than the 49 cc scooters."

At least, I am being saved from the little old lady image with Christine. The row of alternating bikes and scooters no longer looked alien. Step by step I'm getting myself ready to buy a bike. I'm still not certain which one, but I know I can soon make that decision.

I have to ask, "Christine, how long have you been riding and what do you ride?"

Brian laughs. "I've been trying to get her to buy a Goldwing, but she just isn't going for it."

Christine retorts. "A Goldwing isn't right for me unless it is a three-wheeler. Brian likes to tease me. I started off riding an old Kawasaki 750. I had to lean it when I came to a stop because my legs weren't long enough. I went back a step to a Kawasaki 650 because it was just a little shorter. I really didn't like the ride on that one. Next I moved to a BMW because at least then I could balance at a stop. Last year I latched on to a used Honda Silver Wing scooter. I have been diagnosed with arthritis in my right hip. The step through on the Silver Wing has been a treat. I still have enough power to ride with the big boys, but I can easily manage the bike at a stop. That is why I asked you about a used bike. We don't have a used Silver Wing in stock, but we could probably find one if that is what you decide on. So, for now, put yourself on each of these crotch rockets and scooters. Let's see how they feel."

Brian said, "I'll pull each of them out for you so you will have room to get on. I will also steady the bikes as you try them. Just relax, Maggie. We are here for you."

They had probably noticed how nervous I am. I could just see myself knocking over the whole row! "So how large is the engine on this first one?"

"It is a 150 cc and is probably smaller than you want," Brian said. "Let's start with this crotch rocket. It is only 125 cc but is a motorcycle rather than a scooter so it doesn't have the step through."

As I swing my leg over the bike, I knew exactly what Christine was talking about. I didn't have pain in my hip, but the movement was not one that felt comfortable. If I decide on a motorcycle, I'll need a whole new exercise plan! By the third bike, I am fairly certain that I would be happier with the feel of the scooter. I feel more confident when my feet can reach the ground as I get on and off each scooter. I cannot do that with the motorcycles. Denise said I was tall at 5'5" compared to her 5'2". On these bikes, I knew I wasn't all that tall.

Christine asks, "So, Maggie, how did each of these feel? Do you like one over the others?"

"I think I've decided to focus on the scooters. I like being able to steady the bike easily. I still have a lot to consider."

"Come to the back parking lot with me. Let's see what you think of my Silver Wing."

Her bike is silver to match its name. I am nervous once again as I stand it straight and step through. The last thing I want to do is dump her bike on the ground. "This is beautiful. How big is the engine?"

"It is a 600. I can easily cruise the freeways, and even crossing the mountains has not been an issue. I rode to Spokane last weekend to visit friends. It was a wonderful ride. I had considered a three-wheel Goldwing which would help but the leg swing is still an issue. I really want to ride for as many years as I can."

'That sounds like a wonderful plan. Now I have a decision to make. It is not one I intend to rush into. It took me a year to sell my husband's bike, and I couldn't even ride it! I'll get back to you when I decide. If you haven't heard from me in two weeks, please call me. I might need a push."

Brian steps outside to join us. "Well, Maggie, are you going to become a biker?"

I laugh as I answer, "I just may do that." I turn to shake hands with both of them, "Call me if you do get in a used Silver Wing. I'm not sure it is what I want, but I won't rule it out. Thank you both so much for taking so much time with me."

On my drive home, I review all of the scooters I have tried over the last two days. They are all so much alike and yet there are clear differences. How am I ever going to decide?

Chapter Five

My table and counters are covered with motorcycle and scooter brochures when my dear friends Larry and Ed walk into my kitchen a week later. They have been our neighbors for fifteen of the twenty years we've lived in this house. Jim had been a little uneasy when he learned that a gay couple was moving in right next door, but he grew to love them as much as I do. Larry even helped Jim pick out the Goldwing, and now I hope he will help me make a decision.

"Oh, girl, it looks like you are considering doing something really reckless," Ed exclaims. "Please tell me these belong to someone else. Is Richard shopping for a bike?"

"No, they are all mine, but I'm really having a hard time making a decision."

"Is this a scooter? You'd look cute on a nice little scooter. Is this the new style for a Vespa?"

Larry looks over Ed's shoulder, "No, Sweetie. See where it says 650 cc's? That is the engine size. A Vespa scooter is part of the 50 cc or less group. At 650 cc's this is more like an actual motorcycle. My BMW is a 1600, so it is much heavier and faster than this, and mine is designed for long-distance cruising like the Goldwing they rode. I knew about the Honda and Bergman scooters, but BMW makes a big scooter as well? Maggie, are you actually considering buying one of these?"

"I am, but let's have dinner while we talk about it. I made lasagna." The couple started joining us for dinner on Sunday nights when Jim first got sick. They hosted us until he was too sick to leave the house easily, and then usually brought dinner over midweek as well so I didn't have to cook. They've continued the Sunday practice after Jim's death, although I usually cook now. It is nice to have someone else to cook for, and they don't want me to be alone all of the time.

Larry quickly clears the table, making room for the three placemats Ed pulled out. I hand the plates and silverware to Ed as the guys finish setting the table. I think they are as comfortable in my kitchen as they are in their own. Once I add the lasagna and salad, the wine is poured, and we are ready to eat.

Larry offers a toast, "Here is to a new chapter in Maggie's life. May she only ever have good rides."

"Oh dear," Ed adds before taking a sip of wine. "Can't we just toast life or lasagna?"

I smile at each of them. "Let's make the toast to good friends, life, and new adventures. Does that work?" With that, we all join in raising our glasses.

Larry says, "Time to eat. This lasagna smells so good. Yours always comes out better than mine. Of course, I cheat and use canned sauce. I'm not sure I add as much cheese as you do either. Wonderful," Larry said.

Ed spends most of dinner trying to tell me how dangerous motorcycles are, and why neither Larry nor I are in our right minds to even consider it. "The only way I'd ride on a motorcycle is in a sidecar, and even then, they don't build them like a tank. There is nothing to protect you from the cars and the roadway! I thought you two were smarter than that. I thought that when you sold the Goldwing, I wouldn't have to worry about you, Maggie. Why?"

"I understand the why, but why not an actual motorcycle rather than a scooter? I realized that the Goldwing was too heavy and just too much bike, but why not something smaller?" Larry asks between bites of lasagna.

Both men have me laughing at their concerns. "I'm not as strong or flexible as I was at forty, and I know it. Not being 6'1" like you, Larry, means it will be harder for me to handle a motorcycle with my legs around a large gas tank. The scooter models change that and add an automatic transmission so I can concentrate more on riding than shifting gears. That means I will be a little safer, Ed. I may not be an old lady needing a four-wheel scooter, but I think I've really decided that the two-wheel scooter is the way I want to go. Now I just need your help picking the right one. I never knew there were so many different models. They are all the same and yet very different in price and weight. How do I choose?"

Ed announces that he will get the dessert and tea ready to avoid further conversation about me killing myself. Larry just shakes his head, and we restack the scooter brochures separating out all of the regular motorcycles. An hour later, we have eliminated all of the new automatic transmission motorcycles with regular body styles, focusing on just the modified step through designs. Larry is quick to point out that the selections are still extensive if I consider a used bike. Honda no longer produces its Silver Wing, but it had been a popular cruising scooter. I tell them about the one Christine rides. Ed continues to push for nothing faster than a Vespa style. We end the evening with my head spinning. I like to think I am an independent woman, but I really appreciate Larry's input as well as Ed's concern.

For the next two weeks, I find it very hard to join in walks with my friends, and not share my dilemma about buying a bike. They are so supportive of so many things, but this is something I really need to do on my own. I start having imaginary chats with Jim about the merits of each bike. I am rational enough to know I'm having these discussions with myself, but it just seems right to pretend Jim is there for me. I also know that if he were really there to help me make my decision, I would have been more focused and not have changed my mind a dozen times. I think I've finally narrowed down my selection to either a 650 Bergman or one of the three BMW models. That still leaves me with too many selections. I've been back to Hindshaw's three times and the BMW dealer twice. I'm sure they have all muttered about me being a silly woman who can't make up her mind. I'm starting to feel that way myself.

Chapter Six

I have decided that the best way to make a decision is to just put it to the back of my mind and think about other things. Tonight is pizza night at my house with my friends. We try to do this once a month. We can relax in the comfort of my sunroom as we talk without trying to keep up our steady pace as we walk. This is also when Megan shares her latest online dating adventures. We should write a book about the men she has met and rejected. This should take my mind off scooters!

Denise is studying her piece of pizza before announcing, "Do you, ladies, know what I love best about our pizza nights?"

Claire laughs as she reaches for her own piece, "Besides the fact that your son Tyler spends the night with your parents so you could drink as much beer as you want and stay here all night if you need?"

"Or that you get to hear about my love life since you don't have one of your own?" Megan asks.

I step into the group, "Now don't pick on Denise. She knows she can stay here any night even if Tyler is with her, and she will have a love life when she is ready just like the rest of us."

"No, no it is nothing as serious as that." Waiting while she finishes chewing and swallowing the bite of her pizza. "It is simply that I get to have grown-up pizza with fun toppings like mushrooms, chicken, and spinach with white garlic sauce instead of only pepperoni. When do boys start to like something else on their pizza?"

"Well," Megan says with a faraway look on her face. "The last pizza I shared with a man was just three weeks ago. I didn't even bother to tell you about that date.

He had called ahead to order a pepperoni pizza and a pitcher of Budweiser beer without even asking me. Some men just don't get it."

"Wow," Claire says at the same time I say it. "I'll bet you haven't gone out with him again. Now tell us about a good date."

"I can do that, but first, I think I need to tell Maggie about the surprise I have for her. Have you heard about the dating websites for people over fifty?"

Denise is quick to say, "Is that what you use Megan? Is that why you have so many dates with old farts?"

"I do, and many of them are mature professional men, not just old farts. I'll admit that I've found a few of the old farts as well, but I've gotten better at picking through the selections. "

"Yeah, like the pepperoni man."

"I didn't say I was perfect at it. I'm sure if we are all looking at the selections available locally, we can help Maggie find some good ones to date. My surprise is that I've already created your profile, and you have a number of men who have expressed an interest."

I must have looked stricken. Denise puts her hand on my shoulders. "Breathe, Maggie. We want to help you find a date, not call 911 because you stopped breathing. Who knows? If it works out for you, I may try it. This sounds like another reason to love our pizza nights."

Megan turns toward Claire, "Where is Maggie's laptop? We can get her logged in to her new account, and start looking at the profiles of the different men. I think there are some real possibilities there."

I honestly don't know how I feel about online dating. I have heard so many horror stories about women losing their life savings, but I've also heard about people who have found the love of their lives. I don't think I could ever love another man the way I loved Jim. At the same time, I do miss having a man in my life. Ed and Larry are fun, but it just isn't the same. Maybe my friends are correct. Maybe I need to consider dating again. "Okay, let's look at my options."

Claire squeals with delight as Denise throws her head back laughing. "An old fart selection crew."

Megan is quick to correct that. "This will be more like judging for the Olympics."

Denise turns her face away in a grimace, "Oh no, get that image out of my head."

"Well," I insert, "I'm not looking to jump into any type of dating Olympic sports. Discussing life over dinner with a man might be interesting, but I don't plan to go to bed with him!"

Megan says, "Remember the rules. Number One: first date is only for coffee in a very public place like a Starbucks. Second rule: only if you are comfortable with them, do you consent to a dinner date again in a very public restaurant, and only after you have called him at work to confirm that is where he works. Rule number three: if you don't feel comfortable, don't apologize. Say good-bye and just leave. Change the second rule to rule three. Rule two is on that coffee date, make certain that you park your car in a very visible spot, and tell one of us where you are going and who you are meeting. We want you to have a good time but to also stay safe."

"Now you are scaring me."

Claire is quick to give me a hug before saying, "You can do this, Maggie. We are here to help you. First, you have to pick a couple of these men to chat with. We will worry about your dates later. "

We spend the next hour discussing the merits of each of the twelve men who have responded to the profile that Megan created. Some of their responses were just too pushy. Another was an instant reject when he stated that he was looking for a bed partner only. Are there women who would say yes to that? My friends help me draft a reply to three of the men. We sent the same very generic response for all of them. It reads, "Thank you for your interest. Tell me more about yourself." I question if I'll hear from any of them, but time will tell. I had no idea there were so many people over the age of fifty looking for a partner. It seemed so much easier when I was young.

Before we call it a night, I am shocked to have responses from two of the three men. Denise starts laughing as she reads the first reply, "Oh my God. He is looking for a wife who wants to move with him to his brother's farm in North Dakota. He plans to buy a mobile home now while he is still working to park there, and then retire to it in a year or two. Is he serious?"

Claire moves to read over Denise's shoulder, "He goes on that he can't wait to meet you so you can help him select a model with all of the features you would want in the home. This one is an instant reject. Megan, how do you tell them 'No' right away?"

"Well," Megan says with a sigh, "there really isn't any easy way. You can just not reply. I honestly don't think they are waiting breathlessly for a response to every woman they find interesting. Once we've actually met, and I'm not interested in seeing them again, I keep it simple. I say, "It was fun to meet you, but I really don't think we are a good match. I wish you the best." If for some reason I don't say it at the time, I do if they contact me again."

Denise says, "So what do you do in this situation?"

"Knowing how polite Maggie is, I'd vote for a quick "Thank you for your interest, but I don't think we have the same goals for our futures. Or more specifically, I don't see living in North Dakota in my future."

"You are right. I don't see living in North Dakota in my future and think I should tell him so. What did the other one have to say?"

Denise turns back to the laptop, "This one says that he is a commercial real estate developer in Tacoma. He adds that he honestly likes to do all of the things he listed on his profile and hopes to meet a woman who would like to join him. I like this line, 'I think it is important to get to know each other as friends.' Does that mean he doesn't plan to jump your bones, the minute he meets you?"

"Oh my, I sincerely hope none of them intend to do that. I'm not sure I'm ready for this."

Megan squeezes my hand, "Yes, you are. You are going to take a tiny step out of your comfort zone, and have coffee with this man after you've exchanged a few more messages. You need real details like exactly where he works before that coffee date. That way you can have part of your comfort zone with you. You can do this."

Little did my friends know how far I have already pushed my comfort zone as I shop for my bike.

Chapter Seven

Over the next week, I receive six more inquiries from the dating service. The first thing I did after my friends left was to change my password. As much as I love Megan, I do not want her to decide to accept a date from anyone on my behalf. On our next walking trip, she announces that I must be taking the online dating idea seriously because I had changed my password. I just laugh. I do not go into detail about the 'I don't think we are a match' messages that I had sent out to all of the men we had rejected. I remembered when I had sent off my resume in job searches and never heard anything back. I didn't want to treat anyone that way. Most of the men sent back a thank you. One didn't reply. That is okay.

I am still faced with the six new ones as well as the 'Tell me more' replies. I spend two days reading the profiles of those six before sending the 'tell me more' message to two of them and 'I don't think we are a match' to the others. This is getting even more complicated than trying to decide on a bike. I think it is time I ask my friends how I keep all of these men straight.

I start our midweek walk by asking, "Okay, I now have four men I've asked for more information, and all four have replied. I've sent rejections to the rest. I also sent a rejection to Mr. North Dakota. How do I keep all of these men organized in my mind? I never thought I'd have this problem. When you meet someone in person, you either smile or look away. You don't have more than a dozen to remember from their picture and brief description. Megan, how do you do it?"

"Four men? So, Miss Maggie, you are paying attention to the dating site. To be honest, I keep lists in a

Word document. I can move a man from the 'Possible' to the 'Coffee Date, Dinner, More' or to the 'Reject' group. I also place the automatic rejects in a separate group. Some of them will try again later if you stay on the site for more than three months. You are correct that it can get very complicated."

Claire laughs. "I had wondered how you kept them all straight. I bet you have a special group for 'bedroom performance'."

Denise wrinkles up her nose and looks away, "That is just gross. TOO MUCH INFORMATION!! I don't want to picture any of you having sex."

Megan pokes Denise, "Well, I do have sex, but I hadn't considered a rating system. That might be a good idea. Maggie, you love Excel so you could do a database to keep them organized. If I had known how many I would date, I'd have done that rather than my Word system."

Claire points out that Megan could switch to Excel, and that I would be just fine with Word because I won't have that many entries. I take a deep breath, "I think I agree with Denise that a spreadsheet column for performance is way too much, but I will consider putting the information in a list. Two of the men have the first name of Mark, so I'll need to pay attention to which one I'm chatting with." In the back of my mind, I think about using a spreadsheet to organize the information on the bikes I've considered. There I could use a rating column. I need all of the help I can get making a decision on a bike more than I do the decisions regarding the men Megan has added to my life.

I make my spreadsheets for both the men and the bikes. Adding the details about each man and bike has started me thinking about what I think is most important. Tonight as I prepare my dinner, I begin to make two new lists of the qualities that are important to me. The list for the bike is much less painful than the qualities of a man. I've had the perfect man. I'll never find another Jim. Do I start a list with the things I loved most about him, or do I look for things that are the opposite? No, the opposite would never work. I do want to be open to new ideas, but I still need to like the man. I hit the save button as the doorbell chimes. I'm not expecting any of my friends, so it must be a neighbor.

I open the door without glancing out the window. My daughter, Sharon, is standing on my doorstep. "Mother, I'm happy to see that you are locking your door, however, I don't think you looked to see who was here before you opened the door." She continues as she marches in, "That really defeats locking the door when you are home alone. You are alone, aren't you? You really need to consider selling the house so you can move into a condo where there are more people around you and proper security. Of course, I love that you are so close by us." We have moved to the kitchen, where I quickly close my laptop. "You have your laptop in the kitchen? What are you working on here?"

I'm so glad that I selected the 'shut down when closed' option on my laptop as she opens the cover to a blank screen. "I was looking at recipe ideas for my next dinner with Ed and Larry. It is so nice to just list ingredients, and then have recipes pop up that I had never considered. I love my cookbooks, but the internet can be so helpful." *I had best shut my mouth before she starts to think I'm up to something.*

"Well I've come by for two reasons; oh, make that three reasons. The first is that I needed to leave the children with Thomas for a few minutes. They have worn me out today. The second is that I want to borrow your big platter. One of Thomas's banking associates is in town, and we decided to invite him for dinner. Restaurant food can be so tiring when someone is traveling for business." She walks around the kitchen looking at everything on the counter. At least the bike brochures are out of sight in a drawer in the dining room. My daughter can be a snoop. "The third reason is to invite you to join us. Three can be such a difficult dinner party, but I don't want to have too many people for the poor man to meet. Thomas said he is closer to your age than ours, so it will be perfect. I am not trying to be a matchmaker because I know that you aren't interested in dating, and he doesn't live anywhere close. You won't have to worry about him calling you later for dates. Please say you will come."

Wow! I love my daughter, but sometimes she wears me out now as much as she did as a teenager. It may be harder than I had thought to tell her if I really do accept a date for coffee. I don't think she will understand that I was really working on the list of men who have expressed an interest in my online profile. I'll cross that bridge on another day. "Let me get that platter. Did you want the really big one or one of the smaller ones? They are all in the china hutch in the dining room. When do you plan to have him for dinner? Can I bring something?" I walk into the dining room and quickly open the doors on the hutch to keep her from peeking in the drawers.

"I think the one with the squared ends will work perfectly. Will you have time to make your dinner rolls for tomorrow night?"

"Here is your platter, and yes I can make the dinner rolls. What time do you need me?"

"Dinner will be at seven. Thomas said they should be home by 6:30. Will that work for you? I know that sometimes you have late escrow signings."

"I don't have anything in the late afternoon tomorrow so I can be there by 6:30 as well, unless you need my help earlier. What about the children?"

"I have a babysitter coming at 5. She can feed them upstairs in the playroom, give them their baths and tuck them in so I can actually enjoy an adult evening. The idea of wearing a dress without handprints sounds like heaven."

"I remember those days. Moving on, have you had dinner? I was just getting started on mine so I can chop more veggies for you. Do you want a glass of wine? Take a seat at the counter."

"I ate before I came over. I probably shouldn't leave Thomas on his own too long, because I'm sure the girls will wear him out as well. They have been so wired all day. The wine sounds good, but I need to pass." She heads to the door. "Lock the door behind me and remember to look before you open it next time." With that, she is gone, and I need to think about having dinner with her, Thomas, and a man I don't know. A blind date sounds more frightening than a coffee date with a man I have at least seen in a picture and read a description of the things he likes. Well, I do know this man is employed, so maybe I can consider this upcoming dinner as practice for my next step. This may be my turn to answer the question, "Tell me about yourself." Too bad that I won't be able to record my answer. I'll also have to remember to not mention that I am shopping for a motorcycle! I stop in my tracks as I stare at my laptop. I've reduced four men to a list of information on my computer, and I've created another list of qualities that I expect them to have to be part of my life. That is all fine and well for a motorcycle, but I've turned these men into a business type of decision. What am I doing? At this moment I really don't like the way my life is going.

Chapter Eight

Sharon takes her role as the wife of a banker very seriously. She and Thomas selected their house because she felt it was in the 'proper' neighborhood. She goes to the gym regularly to keep her trim shape. They joined the Marine Hills Tennis Club because it was what she thought they should do. When she was young, I did teach her how to set a formal table with crystal and china. I had thought that I would pass all of that on to her once she and Thomas had settled, but I never got that chance. She had registered at all of the department stores so that wedding guests would know her preferences. She was delighted that so many members of Thomas's family had given them place settings as wedding gifts. Her brother Richard had said some very unkind things about her being a snob. I hope she also remembers to have fun, casual get-togethers with their friends. I now reserve my own crystal and china for holidays. They are not the items I use for beer and pizza with my friends or for lasagna with Ed and Larry.

When I arrive the next evening, the house is spotless. Not one sign that two small children live there. The dining room sparkles with the expected china, crystal, and candles. She has removed the leaves out of the large table to make an intimate setting for four. Moving toward the kitchen I call out, "Sharon, the door was unlocked, so I let myself in. Don't you keep it locked when you are home alone?"

"Oh, I knew you would be here a little early, and I don't want Thomas to have to struggle with his keys in front of his guest. Thank you for bringing the dinner rolls in a silver basket. I swear I've run out of serving bowls of the right size. Do you think three vegetable dishes plus roasted potatoes are too much? I also have a salad and a nice roast. I've sliced the roast and will keep it and the potatoes in the oven until seven. I don't know if Thomas planned on cocktails before dinner."

"Sharon, slow down. You have entertained people from the bank before. Why are you so nervous about this dinner?"

"Thomas is up for another promotion. He thinks Mr. Gibson may be in town as part of the committee to make that decision. No one has actually said that, or we wouldn't be inviting him now. But if he is, I want everything to be perfect."

"Just relax and be yourself. I'm sure dinner will be wonderful."

We both turn as Thomas, and his guest stride through the front door. He calls out, "Sweetheart, I'm home." Sharon turns bright pink, making me laugh. At least Thomas remembers to have a little fun as he gives her a quick kiss on her cheek, and then wraps his arm across my shoulders. "Sharon and Mom, I'd like you to meet John Gibson. John, my wife Sharon, and her mother Maggie King."

John and I exchange the customary smiles, handshakes and, the "nice to meet yous". I had not had time to form any expectations from the few things Sharon had shared about this man before he arrived. John can't be more than five feet tall if that and probably weighs in at about eighty-five lbs. My first thought is *I wonder if he shops in the boy's department*. I give myself a mental slap. That is very unkind. I worry that I might crush his hand when we shook. His hands are so tiny. I hear Megan's voice in my head as I glance at his feet. They are half the size of mine, and I know she will remind me of the correlation between shoe size and the size of other parts.

Luckily, Thomas saves me from embarrassing myself. "John and Maggie, would you like a cocktail or a glass of wine before dinner. Sharon says we have about fifteen minutes."

John declines, and I say that I will get a glass of water while I see if I can help Sharon. I hear John and Thomas talking about industry in Seattle as they settle in the living room, and I head into the kitchen. Sharon whispers to me, "Well, I did say that he would not be a man you would need to worry about dating. I had no idea what he looked like."

"What a man looks like will never be important if and when I decide to date. I loved your father for who he was. It didn't hurt that he was handsome, but he was also handsome on the inside. Do you even know if Mr. Gibson is married?"

"I don't know, but I'm sure we will figure that out over dinner. Can you help me dish things up?"

John and Thomas were kind enough to leave their business discussion in the living room as we found our places around the table. Thomas had held Sharon's chair out for her and John did the same for me. He was the first to say, "Sharon, your table and dinner look wonderful." Thomas and I chimed in with our agreement.

I notice that John takes a tiny sampling of everything as we pass the dishes; very polite. I do the same except for the salad. I really wish I could place my salad on my main plate and the other items on the smaller salad plate, but I know Sharon would be more than a little displeased. I do my best to not overload that small plate. John takes note, "So, Maggie, I see that you are a salad lover. Tell me more about yourself."

Okay, here I am at that crossroad. Do I start with my personal life–– 'I am a widow?' Or do I go with business––'I'm an escrow agent?' Businessman and business relationship with Thomas so I reply, "I'm an escrow agent here in Federal Way. I've been with the same company for about ten years. Thomas said that you were here for business with the bank. What do you do?"

"I'm taking over as manager of a new Idaho branch. Boise may not be quite as bustling as Seattle but is far more so than the branch I had in Fairbanks. I'm here because I decided that I wanted to see how other branches handle their day-to-day business."

Sharon smiles as she asks, "How do your wife and family feel about making the move? It must be hard to be so far from friends and family." I swear the little devil really is trying to be a matchmaker, or maybe she wants to point out how unacceptable John might be.

"I moved to Fairbanks after my wife died seven years ago. Most of my extended family lives near Boise, so I'm actually going back home. "

"Oh, that must have been very hard for you. I'm so glad that Thomas and I were here to help Mom after Daddy died two years ago." I wish she recognized the look that I give her, but then she didn't respond to 'the look' when she was a child. How do I stop her now? I just smile.

Thomas steps in, changing the subject. We move on, talking about hobbies, sightseeing, and life in Seattle as well as Boise. Dinner continues on a much lighter note. I am relieved when John asks Thomas to drive him back to his hotel, and I walk home. I now know that I can survive an evening with a strange man, but is that what I want to do? Despite what my friends say, I'm not sure I am ready to date. I will continue to exchange messages with the four men from the dating site. I've reorganized my tracking spreadsheet. All of them have suggested at least once that we need to meet. I am trying to remember what Megan called this stage. Something about scouting for football players comes to mind.

Chapter Nine

I still haven't made a final decision on a bike, but I've narrowed it down to either the Bergman 400 or the Bergman 650. Every evening I review the description of each bike right after I read the inquiries from the dating site. I have made the decision to accept a coffee date with the real estate developer. I am comfortable with the knowledge we can at least discuss the process of buying and selling property. Our office handles more houses than developments, but the escrow details are similar for both. Now, I need to send the acceptance message, and then tell my friends about it. I do hope my friends don't decide that they need to actually be at the coffee shop at that time. If they do, should I acknowledge them and introduce them to my date? This whole thing could be so embarrassing.

I take a deep breath and get ready to start the dating discussion with Denise and Claire as we begin our evening walk. Megan is in LA today. I'm not sure if that is a good thing or a bad because she does have the most experience. I start with last night's dinner party. "Sharon set me up with an almost blind date for dinner at her house last night. He is a business associate of Thomas's who is opening a bank branch in Boise."

Claire frowns, "What in the world is 'an almost blind date' and why would Sharon want to set you up on one?"

Denise jumps in quickly, "You know Sharon well enough to understand the why. She is afraid Maggie is going to start to date, and she wants to control who her mother sees. Sharon likes to control everything. So we are just left with the 'almost blind date' issue."

"Well, I think she wanted it to be a blind date that wasn't likely to be repeated. She knows he is going to live in Boise. The problem is that she hadn't met him, and Thomas really hadn't told her that much about him. His name is John by the way."

Claire starts to laugh, "Okay, what was wrong with him? Is he married with four children?"

"No, he is a widower, and there really isn't anything wrong with him that I know of. I just felt like a giant next to him. He can't be more than five feet tall. I actually had a very unkind thought that he must shop in the boys' department. I just couldn't help it. That thought kept popping into my head as we talked over dinner. I was terrified that Sharon might ask him if he needed one of the children's booster seat that she uses at the table. I was so relieved that Richard wasn't there, because he might have said just that!"

Denise was the first to laugh as she says, "I'll bet if Megan was here, she would want to know about his shoe size. I don't even want to know, but I can guess. So John lives in Boise, and the date will not go anywhere. Next up will be coffee dates with the website boys. Men at that advanced age are probably acting like boys, so I think I'll keep that nickname for them."

"You are terrible. Just remember you aren't that much younger than we are. You are correct, however. I have decided to meet Christopher, the real estate developer for coffee tomorrow afternoon. We will meet at Starbucks in Puyallup on the hill."

"What time? Give me the details about him when we get to the office in the morning. I'll plan to be calling on realtors in that area tomorrow. Denise, what time is your last class? Can you meet me there as well?"

"Now wait just a minute. Megan said I needed to let you know who and where. She didn't say anything about you two chaperoning me. I am fully capable of meeting him for coffee in a public place."

"We know you are, but we will be there as well. Claire, my last class ends at two. Give us a time, so I don't have to wait all afternoon."

"All right, we are meeting at 4:30. Please don't interfere. I'll be just fine."

"Of course you will, and we'll be there to have your back if you need us. We love you, Maggie."

The coffee date is not off to a very good start. He is fifteen minutes late. I am waiting at a table near the window. My friends aren't far away. I recognize him as he parks his Mercedes in two spaces and then struts into the shop. He heads straight for my table, "You must be Maggie. You are even more beautiful in the flesh than you are in your picture. I'm delighted that we are finally meeting. I see you already have coffee. Do you need a refill while I place my order?"

Oh God. This may be worse than dinner with John. "It is nice to meet you, Christopher. I'm good on coffee. Go place your order." *And can you keep on going? How did I not pick up on your attitude in our messages? How old was that picture that you posted? There is no way that you are fifty-seven; eighty-seven might be more like it. Smile Maggie. You can do this. I hope my friends are far enough away so Christopher can't hear their conversation. A quick glance has shown me that their heads are together. I can only guess what they are saying.*

Over the next thirty minutes, Christopher proceeds to tell me how successful his business is, how much he relies on the things that he learned at Harvard Business School where he received his MBA, and how difficult it is to find women who are not just looking for a sugar daddy. He doesn't have to worry about me, because I don't see any 'sugar' in him. I try not to keep looking at my phone as each minute ticks by. Finally, Claire has picked up my unspoken signal and calls me. "Excuse me, Christopher, I really need to take this call. I walk outside so our conversation won't echo in the shop. "Oh, Claire, thank you. I needed an excuse to end this. Let me go back in and tell him thanks, and that I have to leave."

I try to remember to smile as I return to the table to pick up my bag. "Christopher, it was so nice to meet you, but I really have to go. My son needs to have me pick him up. Have a nice evening." With that, I move away as quickly as politely allowable as Christopher continues to talk.

"It was really nice to meet you. I'll contact you soon so we can have dinner. I have a date with a beautiful doctor tonight, but I'll get back to you." By now, I've made it to the door, turning I wave, then head to my car. Claire and Denise are right behind me. My phone rings.

It's Claire again. "There is a sports bar down the block. We want all of the gory details. He looked like an ass."

I have to agree with all of that. Maybe I really don't want to do blind dates. Focusing on the selection of a bike might be a much better use of my time.

Chapter Ten

Two disastrous meetings with 'blind dates' has me questioning the wisdom of even looking at the inquiries I've received on the dating website. I hope there is an easy setting for 'activity suspended' or whatever they call it. Megan said she had paid for three months, but I honestly can't see myself continuing this for that long. At the moment, even three minutes seems, too long. I'll just let it rest for a while, and talk with Megan about this whole thing on our next walk. For now, I intend to focus on my job, my children, my friends, and my bike purchase.

I spend the next two days switching back and forth between the weight of the bike and the power it offers. I have a Saturday afternoon date with Christine at Hindshaws to help me make my final decision.

The morning of our walk, I waste no time asking Megan for help with the online dating. I really don't know what I want to do about it. "Megan, I need your expert advice. Claire and Denise will give you all of the details about my awful meeting with the real estate developer. I'm not sure I'm cut out for the online dating thing. How do I put the website on Do Not Disturb?"

Megan laughs and gives me a quick hug, "Claire sent me messages right after your coffee date, and Denise had done the same about your dinner at Sharon's. We don't need to rehash that if you don't want to." We continue our walk. "So you want to back off for a while. I remember that I felt that way before I bought my condo. I would look for a couple of weeks and then take a break for a couple more weeks. It would get just too overwhelming. You can do the same at the dating site. Just ignore it. Some of the men who have been interested will drop out. Others will replace them. You also have the option to review the men that are out there, and you can contact them. Just relax. From the sounds of it, you deserve a break."

Denise says, "I don't think I'll ever consider online dating. You have shown me that my concerns are real. Of course, I'd be looking at much, much, much younger men. Hopefully, that group wouldn't be ninety trying to pass themselves off as forty-five."

"I really don't think he was ninety," Claire said. "But he had clearly misrepresented his age. I don't envy any of you trying to date. My husband may be a jerk at times, but as the saying goes, I do have a date on major holidays. After all of these years, I know what to expect from him."

Megan, Denise, and I sneak a quick glance out of the corner of our eyes at each other. None of us think she has any bargain in her husband, but we don't say it. I'd really like to make a joke about him just being a jerk all of the time, but I can't think of a good way to say it. Sometimes, it really is best to ignore things.

It is hard not to tell my friends about my plans for the afternoon. Reviewing my spreadsheet for the two bikes over lunch at home still has me going back and forth between the Bergman 400 and the 650. Well, today will be the day. It's time for me to head down the hill to Hindshaw's once more.

Christine and Brian are waiting for me as soon as I walk into the store. We head to the back lot where both models are parked. Christine has me get on each of them, and as I pull the 400 to an upright position, she says, "Gently rock it from one side to the other. Don't try to tip it like you are going into a turn, but just as you might once you come to a stop. Use your legs to take the weight." I follow her instructions.

"I can feel the heaviness, the weight, but it is not as heavy as I remember the bike in the training class Jim and I took. I hated that bike."

"Now do the same thing with the 650. It will be heavier by about one hundred forty pounds."

Switching to the bigger bike makes me nervous. *Oh God, I don't want to drop it.* "It's heavier, but it feels more stable or am I just imagining that?"

Brian steps in, "You're right, the back tire is just a little larger and the wheelbase is ten inches longer. It spreads the weight out."

Christine hands me a helmet. "Let's have you move back to the 400. I'm going to have you take a short ride to the end of the parking lot. Remember to apply the brakes equally. Keep your speed just slow enough to keep the bike upright and moving forward."

"You're going to actually let me ride it!"

Brian laughs. "We normally don't allow test rides, but the manager agreed that it was an important part of helping you make a decision. I'll walk down to meet you at the other end." With that, he walks off.

I must look as terrified as I feel. Christine gives me a big smile. "Just relax. You will need to move the kickstand up to fire up the bike. Unlike a motorcycle, you can't rev up the engine unless you have both brakes on fully. Because this is an automatic transmission, giving it gas tells it you are ready to go. Squeeze your brakes as you push forward a little with your feet. Now Brian is in place. Are you ready? Gently give it some gas. Off you go."

Concentrating on going slow and moving forward, my instinct is to keep my feet out so I can touch the ground if I need to. I put them on the floorboards just before I start to brake at the end of the lot and quickly put them back out. The bike stops easily. "Wow, that was both fun and frightening. I like it. Now, what do I do?"

Brian helps me set the kickstand down. "Do you want to ride it back or do you want to walk back to get the 650?"

"I think I'll walk, so I remember to breathe again," I say with a laugh.

"Fair enough. I'll move this one out of your way. See you in a few."

As I started to walk away, I realized that not only did I need to catch my breath, but I needed to unclench my hands. I had gripped the handlebars for dear life. Even my legs were still a little shaky. I didn't want to make my decision on 'you break it, you buy it.'

I can't decide if I am more confident as I settle on the 650, or less so knowing how much more power I was holding. I'll try to remember to breathe this time. Christine gives me a thumbs up, "You can do this. Go for it, girl." I close my eyes for a minute to relax and start forward. I move my feet up and in just seconds back down as I brake to stop beside Brian.

Carefully setting the kickstand before I dismount, I hand the helmet to Brian as I smile. "I've found my bike. I want the 650. Let's get Christine so we can write up the deal. How much wiggle room is there in the price?"

"We will make you the very best deal that we can. Congratulations. Maggie King, Biker Woman!" I can hear Christine laughing just before we join her. At least he didn't call me a biker chick!

Chapter Eleven

Later that evening, I call my motorcycle friend and neighbor. "Larry, I've purchased my bike. It is the Burgman 650. It is an attractive charcoal gray color and very powerful. I'm so excited."

We continue to chat about the features of my new bike. "So it is gray, and you had wanted red. Red would suit you, but I'm sure you will let the world know you are a woman having fun on that bike." I knew from our Goldwing shopping that motorcycles do not come in the same array of colors that are available for cars. Hindshaw's did get in a used 2010 Honda Silver Wing in Candy Apple Red, but that bike had almost 150,000 miles on it! Someone had really loved it.

"I will just have to settle for a bright red helmet."

"A red helmet will work for you. Ed, of course, would probably vote for shocking pink. You are very much a lady, even on a motorcycle."

"Now, I have a very important question to ask."

With my decision made, purchase transacted, and check written, I am now faced with getting the bike home. I have just purchased a bike I am not ready to ride! Jim and I had taken the motorcycle safety classes before we bought the Goldwing. Jim had gotten his license endorsement, but I had only wanted to be a better backseat rider. I didn't even take the final riding test. I will need to retake the class and pass. I could put the bike on the trailer I had used for the Goldwing, but I have decided I would rather have Larry ride it home for me. I'd really like to ride on the back, but that might be risky until he is comfortable with how that bike handles. At least he can park it in my garage for me.

That way, I can go out to look at it as I read the owner's manual. I'm sure Larry will tease me about that just as he did when I read the owner's manual for my new laptop computer.

"What is that?"

"Could you ride it home for me? I'll need to get my endorsement, but I don't have that yet."

We agree on a time for the next day. I call my friends to make sure they will all be there for our evening walk. All I tell them is that I have some exciting news.

Even before I can get out of my car, Megan rushes to open the door and pull me out. Denise and Claire are right behind her. "I knew you could do it, Woman. So, you've actually found a man you like. Congratulations." With that, she gives me a big hug. "Now tell us all about him."

I have to laugh, "Let me tie my shoe and lock my car so we can get started on our walk." I wonder how far I can take this as a joke before telling them the truth. Probably not as far as Megan would. "Well, he is not overly tall or heavy. He just fits right in all of the important places. The gray is dignified and classy rather than dull and boring. The power is delightful, but I still feel I'm in control. It will take some practice, but I can't wait to really ride him. It is just so exciting."

Claire stops in the middle of the walking path, "Maggie King, are you really talking about a man? This just doesn't sound like you at all!"

Doubling over in laughter at my own joke, it takes me a minute before I can speak. All of my friends look at me like I've lost my mind. "You are correct, Dear Claire. I am not talking about a man. I've just purchased a Bergman 650 scooter. It is gray, sleek, and very powerful. I really can't wait to be able to ride it."

Megan tries to not smile and assumes a thoughtful poise with her fist resting under her chin. "A motorcycle might be as much fun as a man. You can wrap your legs around it, hugging him tight as you ride him. And you would be in total control as you should be with a man. The scooter won't keep your bed warm at night, but it might be a good way to meet a man who can do just that."

"I did not buy the bike as a way to meet men. I just want to be able to enjoy riding. Jim and I had so much fun. It won't be the same, but some parts of it that I enjoyed I can experience on my own. I have also decided that I'm not interested in shopping for a man online. I may change my mind later, but I'm too old school for that. I just cannot do blind dates. I admire you, Megan, that you can do that. I just can't. Now let's talk about something else. Megan, where were you this week?"

Megan gives me a quick hug and whispers in my ear, "You are right that blind dates can be awful, but the option is there for you later if you change your mind."

Megan delights us with stories about her men in Memphis. She does get around.

The next night Larry rides the bike home and says it is faster than he expected. Ed joins us as the ladies arrive with dinner and wine. After showing off the bike, we move to the dining room. The smell of Chinese food has my stomach growling. Everyone grabs a plate and dishes out food from the boxes as we move around the table.

Larry proposes a toast, "To Maggie and her new bike. Good rides ahead." Cheers fill the room.

The women are all disappointed that I had not invited them to join me when I bought the bike. Megan, as always, asks about the men in the store. Claire wants to know if I have seen the grubby Harley Man, and Denise asks when we were going shopping for my new helmet and riding gear. We make plans to meet at Destination Harley in Tacoma after work the next day. Megan flies out in the morning but says she will check in later to see how things go. Denise asks that Claire and I not embarrass her, but that doesn't mean she won't join us. Ed and Larry state that they will pass because they aren't shopping for new men but wish us all luck. Once again, I remind all of them that I am shopping for riding gear, not men. Tomorrow night should be fun; another new adventure. For now, I please myself with the fact that I have a hot Bergman scooter waiting for me in the garage.

Chapter Twelve

Destination Harley has two stores, one in Tacoma and the other on the opposite side of Puget Sound in Silverdale. Both are all about motorcycles of any brand, but the Harleys are all front and center. They have row after row of new and used bikes, a large parts and service department, and equally large corner for riding gear and accessories. I had purchased some of my riding gear here when Jim bought the Goldwing. All of that had been sold at the estate sale for Jim's things. I had gone to the beach that weekend, and let others handle the sale. This was a fresh start and time for new gear.

Claire walks in rubbing her hands together, stating loud and clear, "Now what looks yummy?"

Rolling her eyes, Denise is the first to smile at a man standing in front of a Harley Sportster. "We could start with him," she whispers.

As I turn to look, the man heads out of the store. I'm shaking my head as I reply. "Number one, the Sportster is the low powered, lower-priced model, so I think you want one with more class. And two, that is probably the grubby man from the Honda store I told you about."

"Grubby or not that is one nice long pair of jeans and a great ass. He fills the bill for me as Mr. Harley Man," Denise says.

Just then my phone rings. I see it is Megan calling. "Is everything all right? You don't usually call until it is time for you to pick up your dog."

"I only called to tell you I've arranged for you to start the motorcycle safety class Thursday night. Class starts at 6 PM, and then will run 8 AM to 6 PM Saturday and Sunday. I'll be back home this weekend so you won't have to worry about Muffin. Tell everyone hi for me and have fun shopping." Before I can thank her, she has ended the call. Wow, she didn't waste any time on getting me started on actually riding my new bike.

The riding apparel department is divided into sections for men and women. I begin looking at helmets while the ladies start pulling out leather pants. They announce they want to help me find things that were sleek and sexy. "How about a pair of chaps? They would really highlight your butt the same way they do for the cowboys in those westerns."

"Motorcycle gear needs to protect my butt, not play it up. Jeans help, but I really want to protect my skin if I dump my bike. Look for a pair of medium weight full leather pants in my size."

The poor saleswoman is having a hard time trying to answer questions in three directions as Denise heads over toward the jackets. Of course, the woman looks a lot like the stereotype of a "biker chick" – twenty-five, curvy, long dark hair pulled into a thick braid, small tattoo on her wrist and wearing skin-tight jeans, equally tight T-shirt and a leather vest. Her laugh sounds sincere as she listens to the running dialog between the three of us. "You need a jacket with lots of snaps and zippers. Didn't Marlon Brando wear that type, or was it on the men in Easy Rider? We really need to set up a motorcycle movie fest after you pass your class."

"No, no, I think we need to watch the riding portion of her class. Think of all of the possibilities there. We can help her pick out some good ones. Sounds like more fun than being in the ladies' section of a testosterone store."

"I don't want a leather jacket for this summer. I want a vented First Gear model with a zip-out lining so I have the options for cool mornings or warm afternoons," I call out.

"Boring!" is shouted from both of my friends. *What am I going to do with them? Shouldn't I be the trouble maker here? I am the one with a new motorcycle.*

The saleswoman shows me the group of mesh jackets in both short and long styles. I find the perfect jacket with cool mesh sleeves, armor in shoulders and elbows and purple, fuchsia, and black panels. The ladies both give it a thumbs-up. I can be safe but still stand out from the sea of black leather and denim.

Despite all of the help, I manage to select pants, jacket, and helmet. The helmet is in my chosen bright red. The jacket may not match my red helmet but isn't that the idea at this age? As we head to the checkout, Denise stops at a rack of do-rags. She holds up one in a bright yellow. "This is the final touch to have you qualify for the Red Hat Society. They also have it in purple so you can switch and still make your statement."

This is what friends are for.

Washington State, like all other states except Alabama, requires a special test for a motorcycle license called an endorsement. There is a written test for a permit followed by a riding skills test. The motorcycle safety class covers both tests as part of the program. I had passed the written portion before, and had learned to ride the smaller motorcycles provided for the class, but had elected not to take the riding skills test. I really should have taken the "never ridden" version of the class, but Jim and I had wanted to take the class together. He had ridden bikes as a teenager when an endorsement was not required. He felt he needed the safety refresher as well as earning the endorsement. My goal was to have learned enough to be a good back seat rider. I needed to learn how to lean into a corner rather than leaning the opposite way, which was my first reaction. It took me a while to be confident that the bike would not fall over. I may have watched Tom Cruise riding those bikes around lots of sharp, fast curves, but my stomach said it was just plain wrong. The class helped me learn that but, now things have changed. I need to learn to ride and to pass that skills test. I'm so thankful that Megan had made the call. With a permit, I can be legally riding by Friday and feel better about doing so by Monday.

As expected, the classroom at the mall in Auburn on Thursday evening is filled with men. Most of them looked to be under thirty, but a couple of them are well past that age. I am surprised to see our "Harley Man" leaning against the wall in the front of the room. I'm even more surprised to have him nod in my direction, although I can't see his eyes through his dark glasses. Did he actually remember me? The ladies might be right, this might be entertaining, but he is really not a man who would interest me. He still looks grubby in his old leathers and scraggly beard. I'm only there to get my endorsement, not check out a prospect as Megan calls them. Before he takes a seat in a back corner, he says a few words to the other man at the front.

Promptly at six, the instructor introduces himself, passes out instruction books, and starts a sign-in sheet around the room. He asks each of us to introduce ourselves, and our riding experience. Once we have all done that, the Harley Man is still in the back and has not introduced himself. Our instructor acknowledges him as a future instructor who will be observing but does not call him by name. The class time goes quickly, and I forget all about the mystery man in the back. The evening ends when we all pass the written portion of the class. Class will meet again for the skills practice at 8 AM on Saturday. As I head toward my car, I see Mr. Harley Man's Road King roar out of the parking lot. Good thing I didn't want to get to know him. I have to admit I am curious about him. Everyone has a story, and I'm sure his is a great one.

Saturday and Sunday turn into long days getting to know the clutch on my assigned 350 cc Kawasaki bike. They usually have a scooter available, but it is in the shop. I don't want to know why it is there. Neither the idea of a mechanical failure nor an accident makes me feel confident at the moment. I can't say that the Kawasaki is my friend, but it is doing the job. I could have asked for permission to bring my own bike but didn't feel comfortable riding it to class. I have too much to learn first. We start by pushing our bikes across the parking lot before pushing one another as we learn to balance and to put our feet down safely. I am paired with a rather large older man. He has no difficulty pushing me, but I am exhausted by the time I get him across the lot. The instructor lets me catch my breath by throwing in a quick safety lesson.

"Mrs. King, park your bike and come over here, please." *How can I be in trouble already? Is he going to ask me to leave class just because I'm the only woman and old as well?* "Mrs. King is wearing proper riding gear. The leather pants will protect her if she dumps her bike. All of you need to assume you will dump your bike at least once. She also has selected a full-face helmet which provides maximum protection to both her head and her face. Her jacket has armor in all the right places, but even more importantly, it has bright colors that will allow car drivers to see her just a little easier. It would be better if it were bright yellow or lime green, but I know this style doesn't come in those colors. The purple and pink tells the drivers, she is female and just a little safer. Thank you, Mrs. King."

"Please call me Maggie." Starting up the bikes and having the rest of Saturday with the engine operating is a relief. By the time we return to the classroom for more safety lessons, I am thinking about a hot bath, glass of wine, and bed. This has not been a fun-filled day.

Sunday starts at 8:00 AM, and I have tried to balance enough coffee to get me going and not so much that I'd spend all morning dreaming about a restroom. More riding skills practice ends at lunch. Sunday afternoon is all about the skills testing. Mr. Harley Man has been standing to the side, silently observing once again. He is as grubby as before, and the mirrored sunglasses look like they are a permanent fixture on his face. How can someone who looks that grubby be an instructor? I am ecstatic when I pass the test, although I did murder a cone on the weave test. I am beating myself up about it when one of the guys murders two cones and another just one. The group is very jubilant when the instructor announces that we have all passed with good scores. The men decide to head out for beer and pizza. I wish them luck, but tell them that I am heading home. Mr. Harley Man is already riding out of the lot. We had not exchanged a word during the two days. The ladies will be disappointed. I am too, but not for the same reasons. He is either a mystery or just a puzzle. Either way, I really wish I knew more about him simply because I have seen him so often.

Chapter Thirteen

I turn my phone on as I park in my driveway. Five messages from my children is not a good sign. Hopefully, there is nothing seriously wrong. Most of the messages are from Sharon asking where I am, and if I am okay. I return the call to my daughter. "Hi, Sharon, I just got home. I'd had my phone off."

"Mother, where are you? Are you okay? Richard and I have not been able to reach you all weekend. I didn't think anything about it Saturday evening, but you didn't call me back. We've been frantic. I wanted to call the police, but Richard said to wait. We are coming over right now. We need to talk. I can't handle this."

Before I can say a word, she hangs up. I had planned to tell my children about my bike, but this wasn't how I expected the conversation to start. When did my children forget that I'm their parent and a grown woman who is trying to have a life?

True to her word, Sharon and Richard are there just after I pull the car into the garage. There are times when I wish she and her husband, Thomas, had purchased a house a little farther away. Thomas isn't with them, which means he is home with the girls. Sharon has a look of shock on her face as she steps out of her car, and Richard has a little smile.

"Mother, why are you dressed in motorcycle gear? I thought you sold Daddy's motorcycle? Whose bike is that in the garage? Do you have a boyfriend and is that his bike in there? Is he the one who is forcing you to do stupid things like riding a motorcycle at your age? It was bad enough when Daddy decided to do that, but I'd hoped you were past that silliness."

"Sis, it is Mom's bike. It is not actually a motorcycle but a scooter. I saw the brochures on her counter last week and didn't think I should be the one to tell you. A big scooter is a good selection for you, Mom. How fast will this baby go? So you decided to go with the bigger model Bergman. I'd have thought that you would go with the 400. It is a lot lighter. By the way nice riding gear."

It seems safer to start with Richard's questions first. Sharon's mouth is still hanging open, so I'll have a minute or two before she starts in again. "I thought about the 400 and even the 250 but decided that the 650 would be a better choice on the highway. Larry said he hit eighty coming up the hill from Auburn when he rode it home for me. He warned me that it has lots of pick up. He doesn't want me to get a ticket my first time out." I try to laugh, hoping it will ease the tension. Richard gives me a silly grin. He knows what I am trying to do.

"Wow! That is great. You should be able to cross the mountains and merge on the freeways without an issue. So, have you not ridden it yet? Were you going out now? Sharon said you just got home."

"I've been at the motorcycle safety class relearning how to ride all weekend. I passed my test, so I am street legal. I'll need lots of practice before I start riding regularly. Let's go inside and pour all of us a glass of wine while we catch up."

Richard holds the door for us. I swear Sharon is stomping like she did so often as a teenager. Maybe this means I'll get to be the parent again in this discussion. Richard quickly leads the way to the kitchen, opens the wine, and fills our glasses. Sharon is leaning against the counter with her arms crossed over her body.

By this time, she has recovered her voice. Her face is still flushed. She pushes her long blonde hair off her shoulder and puts her hands on her hips. She looks a lot like she did as a six-year-old lecturing Richard for flattening her sandcastle. She doesn't even take a sip of her wine before she starts in using her best child lecture voice. "Richard, don't encourage her. She is fifty-five years old and should not be taking up such a dangerous hobby. It was bad enough when she was riding with Daddy, but on her own bike is ridiculous. Mother, think about your grandchildren. What will their friends think about you dressed like a twenty-year-old biker chick? Daddy would roll over in his grave if he saw you and knew what you were doing. I thought you were going to use the money from the sale of Daddy's bike to take a nice cruise somewhere warm. At least there if you wanted to meet men, they would be safe and sane rather than some criminal in a bike gang. Ed and Larry knew about this, and didn't try to talk you out of it?"

I shake my head and take a deep breath before I respond, "Slow down, Sharon. Your father would not be rolling in his grave. He would have both of his feet in the middle of my back telling me to get on that bike and enjoy it. I'm also not interested in meeting men of any type for anything other than friends. Ed, of course does not like the idea, but Larry at least understands. Your dad and I tried to explain to you why we liked riding when we bought the Goldwing. You've never done it, so you just don't understand how it makes me feel. I'm not trying to embarrass you or my grandchildren, but I need to live my life on my terms, Sharon. I have tried to let both of you do the same. You need to respect that."

"Come on, Sis, let's go. Mom looks tired, and you are not helping anything. We can go back to your house where you can vent at Thomas and hopefully get this out of your system. Love you, Mom, and I'll come over for dinner some night this week. Does Thursday work for you?"

"Thank you, Sweetie. Thursday will work just fine. Sharon, I'll talk to you in a day or two, but I really don't want to discuss my bike with you again. I love you both."

"Well, I hope that if anyone gets things out of their system, it will be you and this motorcycle nonsense. Thomas is never going to believe this."

I almost feel sorry for both Richard and Thomas. I know that my daughter is not likely to give up on this discussion anytime soon. How did I raise a daughter who is so conservative? Neither Jim nor I were ever like that. We both had a few wild days before we settled into paying a mortgage and changing diapers. Richard seems to be exploring life, but Sharon has never wanted to do that. I'm too tired to worry about that now. Dinner, bath, and bed right after I call my friends to let them know I passed my skills test! I now have a motorcycle endorsement! Look out Bergman. We are ready to hit the streets or more likely a parking lot for lots of practice. Maybe I'll think of a good name for the bike as I soak in the tub. Should it be a male or a female name? Silly or more intellectual? Good grief, I always have had trouble coming up with a good name for a cat. How am I going to decide on a name for the bike? "Murphy Jones" works just fine for the cat although "James Garner" would have worked as long as I was not going to shorten it to "Jim". One Jim in the house would have been enough. This could take some serious thought which probably won't happen tonight.

Chapter Fourteen

Having passed my skills test means that I know how to ride a small motorcycle. Now I need to practice those same skills on my own bike. I remember that Jim had taken the Goldwin to a local parking lot to do lots of slow turns before he even thought about having me on the back. We repeated that time at the parking lot when I did climb on. He had said that the balance was more difficult when going slow than it was racing down the highway. It seemed to work for him, so I plan to do the same thing. I have rearranged my work schedule so I'll have a little more time each morning for a practice ride. Before 8 AM the parking lot of the Fred Meyer store is almost empty. I should have most of the side lot clear, so I can use the parking space lines as practice cars. Repeating the stops, turns, and weaves we had done in class over and over again will help me feel more confident. The best part is that the store is only a few blocks from the house, and I can ride the back streets to get there.

By the third morning, I am actually starting to feel good about the turns and stops. The weaves are still a little tricky. As I come to another stop, a tall, well-dressed middle-aged man comes out of a side door and walks over to me. I am sure he is going to ask me to leave their lot. I shut down the bike and remove my helmet, so I can hear him.

"Hi, I'm Mike Smith, manager of this store. Is that actually a scooter rather than a motorcycle?"

I give him a big smile. His voice is deep with a hint of a Southern drawl. "Mike, I'm Maggie King, and yes this is a scooter. I just got my motorcycle endorsement after buying the bike." I realize I'm talking way too fast. I hope he doesn't notice just how nervous I am. I really want to be able to do more practice riding here in the lot. "I don't live very far from here and wanted to practice before I actually headed out on the road for a serious ride."

"I've seen you in the store. Coming here this early seems like a good idea for practice. Of course, I can't really say that. I ride myself, but I'm sure the company has regulations somewhere in my manual about not encouraging motorcycle riding in the parking lot. Did you take the class?"

"I did this past weekend."

"They introduce you to some really good skills. I wanted to have them set up a course here in the lot, but the company vetoed that idea. Corporate was very worried about our liability," he adds. "People who don't ride don't always understand that it does take practice."

"What do you ride Mike?"

"Oh, I have a Kawasaki 750 that I've had forever. It does not look as good as yours. You also look really sharp in your red helmet and that fancy jacket. The bright pink should help drivers see you. I wear a basic black leather jacket."

"So, are you chasing me out of your parking lot?"

"Oh no, we will pretend I haven't seen you, but if you swing by when you are done, I'd love to buy you a cup of coffee."

"It is time for me to head home for a shower before work, but let's try the coffee another morning."

As I ride off, I realize the ladies will be proud of me. I almost made a date with a good-looking man. He is probably married, but will wonders never cease? Best of all, I can continue my practice.

Chapter Fifteen

Over the next two weeks, I continue to practice in the parking lot most mornings. I've added quick rides the length of the parking lot before coming to a stop as part of my regular routine of slow weaves and curves. On Saturday morning, I spot Mike Smith watching me once again. I park my bike and pull off my helmet as I walk over to talk to him. "Morning, Mike. Have you come to chase me out yet?"

"No, not at all. You are getting much better at your practice drills. I realized that you will soon be leaving the practice behind to hit the streets for real. I wanted to see if you will be here tomorrow so that we could finally have that cup of coffee. I'd suggest that we do that today, but Saturdays are just too unpredictable for me to make the time this morning. What do you think?"

I have mulled over the idea of having coffee with Mike since he first suggested it. To do so doesn't seem like it is in the same league as those disastrous blind dates of a few weeks ago. I've met him and know where he works. I don't need to call my friends about having coffee with him as a precaution to keep myself safe. It might be interesting to chat with him as a new friend. This doesn't need to be complicated.

"Tomorrow morning sounds good. You are correct that it may very well be my last morning in your parking lot. I try to finish by eight. Is that too early for you?"

"No, it isn't too early. I like to vary my schedule to give me the chance to work with all of my employees during the week. Does the Starbucks here work for you? I'm sure my staff will tease me later, but that is okay. I like to keep them guessing."

With our time set, I return to my bike to ride out of the lot. I did tell a white lie. I had planned to have today be my last day of practice drills. I honestly think I'm ready to try more of a real ride. Now, however, I need to go home to change before meeting my friends for our morning walk.

Claire starts our discussion on the walk. "My husband, Mike, is making comments about his boss. I really hope he doesn't quit his job again. I have just about gotten all of my charge cards paid off from the last time he quit. Why does he think he only needs to work for six months a year and then spend the next six loafing at home?"

She has asked this question so many times. It is hard to even try to say something that will help her through this once again. I so want to tell her to just kick his ass out. Claire is such a warm, loving woman. She deserves to be treated like a queen rather than as a doormat. "I'm so sorry, Claire. I really hope he keeps this job a little longer. I know how hard it is for you when he is unemployed."

"Oh, I don't want to talk about this again until it actually happens. Okay, ladies tell me something fun. Megan, any hot new dates? Maggie, any online prospects?"

Megan is quick to give us an update. "I was back in LA this week. I don't have online connections there yet. I did agree to have dinner with one of my clients. Big mistake. He kept trying to have me drink more wine while he finished the bottle. Even while we were in the restaurant. he would try to pull me close for a kiss or a grope. When we left the restaurant, I tried to get him into one cab while I took another. It didn't work. He was all over me like flies on shit. I thought about pulling out my can of mace. By the time we reached my hotel, he was mumbling that his wife was going to kill him. I thought about doing just that. I thought for sure I'd lose his account."

Staring at Megan in shock, Denise says the same thing I am thinking, "You seem so good at keeping your dates in line. How did that one get so out of hand?"

"I'd like to say that it was just that he got drunk. I had no idea that he would be like that. I only ever have one glass of wine on a date. I do like to be in control, and I'm so glad that is what I did that night. I would hate to wake up to a man with a hangover muttering about his wife."

Claire asks, "What did you do with him when you reached your hotel?"

"I paid the cabbie who helped me get him out of the cab and into the lobby of the hotel. The desk clerk there had the barkeeper bring him coffee. By the time I came down in the morning, he was gone."

I ask, "Did you lose his account?"

"Nope. He said he didn't remember what happened after we had dinner. He remembered drinking coffee until some desk clerk in some hotel called a cab to take him home. He asked if I got back to my hotel okay, and did he owe me for cab fare? I didn't know what to say. I will never mix business and pleasure again. There was not a bit of pleasure there. Okay, Miss Maggie, what about your love life?"

"I don't have a love life and may never have one. I quit looking at the online site. I just can't see myself doing the blind dating. I just can't. I have been practicing on my scooter at the Fred Meyer store almost every day. Tomorrow after I finish my practice, I have agreed to have coffee with the manager. I think we can be friends."

Megan says, "That is a good step, but you have male friends like Larry and Ed. You need a man who can kiss you until your toes curl. Every woman deserves that at every stage of her life. Now tell us more about the manager."

"You'll have to wait until tomorrow evening's walk before I'll be able to tell you more. The only thing I know is that he has a motorcycle and that he is the manager at that store. Be patient."

Chapter Sixteen

Coffee with Mike Smith was pleasant. He is a nice man. We talked about our children, his ex-wives, and our bikes. He suggested that we do a ride and then dinner somewhere away from his store. That might be fun. My friends seemed disappointed when I tell them about him during our evening walk. They are all hoping I will get my toes curled. Not going to happen.

Larry calls a week later. He suggests we try an actual ride on Saturday down to Salty's restaurant in Redondo for lunch. I've made a few rides around town, but I am ready for more. He knows I can never turn down Salty's. Their seafood is always great, but sitting out over Puget Sound is just too good to ever pass up. He thought that an early lunch would have a little less traffic, and it is only a short distance but still a real ride. This would give me practice riding down a hill with lots of curves, which means I have to go slow and steady. Having Larry near will make me feel much better than trying this all on my own in case I do something stupid like drop my bike. Ed says he will meet us there. I know he really thinks we are both nuts.

The April weather is perfect, sunny and seventy-two degrees. The air smells first of flowers and then the sea as we drop down to Redondo Beach. The smells are something that makes riding a bike so special. The beach is located just north of Federal Way but south of Des Moines. There are so many beautiful beaches in this area, but Redondo is one of my favorites because of Salty's. Larry parks his BMW bike near the door, and I share the parking space. Ed parks his car nearby. Larry wants to know how I feel about my riding ability, and Ed rolls his eyes. He knows that will always get me laughing.

"I'm starting to feel more comfortable. Riding in the parking lot has helped a lot. I think I'm really ready to challenge myself. Now that I know I can go down a steep hill, I may be ready to head down the hill to Auburn. The road to Flaming Geyser State Park might be fun. I'm not quite ready but soon. In a week or two, I may even be ready to ride to work."

"Why is that so special?" Ed asks as we are shown to our table beside the window.

"Well, it means that I have to be prepared to ride both directions no matter how tired I am after a full day of work or how much traffic there might be. That could be difficult. If it is one of the evenings I join my girlfriends for our evening walk in Kent, I would still need to be ready to make that ride home. Right now, riding takes a lot of concentration and even more energy."

"More riding on the open road will help you relax, although you will always need to concentrate while you are on your bike. That is what ensures a safe ride. You might want to look for a scooter rider's group or maybe join in on one of the group rides from Destination Harley in Tacoma to their store in Silverdale. I've done a few of those rides with a group of men. It is a nice trip, and everyone has been great. I'm sure your scooter will be accepted as well as my BMW was. Not all Harley riders mock other bikes."

I tell the guys about the cool response I had received from the mysterious Harley Man, and then we discuss the riding groups. "There is an online scooter riders group that I might join. They should be a good resource if I have questions, but they would not be people I can ride with. The Seattle scooter riders all ride small 50 cc models around town and would be more like the rides from the movie *Larry Crowne*. "

Ed gets a big smile on his face. "I loved that movie. If you two rode that kind of scooter, I'd ride with you. Now, that looked like so much fun."

Larry pats Ed's hand and says, "I know you liked that movie. I actually think that you and Maggie both have a crush on Tom Hanks. Maggie needs a group that can go faster than thirty-five miles an hour. A rider's group for her may need to include actual motorcycles. There are a number of women who ride the smaller Harleys. Some of them are a little wild, but others are more ladylike. You are in a class by yourself. You know, Maggie, if I were looking for a woman, you would be my first choice. I'm never going to be looking, but you are special as well as beautiful. You also have perfect hair because you never seem to have helmet hair even after taking off your do-rag."

Ed chimes in "You do have wonderful silver hair. That short cut really works for you. I've always wondered how that head wrap bandana got the name "do-rag". Is it really because it protects your hairdo?"

The waitress joins the conversation as she drops off our check. "I actually looked that up on Wikipedia just the other day. You are right because it does come from hairdo. Doesn't seem to fit for a bald guy." With that, she moves on to another table.

"See, Ed, the world wants to help you learn about motorcycles and motorcycle gear."

With lunch over, Ed heads to his car as we walk to our bikes. Ed said he did not want to watch us ride out. Before we could do so, a familiar Harley Road King roars into the parking lot. After pulling off his helmet, the Harley Man nods in my direction. Once again, he looks grubby with his longish hair and his eyes hidden behind his sunglasses. Pulling down my visor, I ride out without acknowledging him. Larry follows right behind me.

As soon as we pull into our driveways, Larry strides over to ask me about the Harley Man. Ed joins us. I try to explain, that although I am seeing the man everywhere, I really don't know him. Larry is quick to fill Ed in on what he had seen. "The man was tall with a nice smile and rides a great bike. When he pulled off his helmet, all I could think of was Sam Elliot with a mustache, long graying hair and three-day beard. Maggie, you really need to pay more attention when a good-looking man shows you some interest. I'm in a committed relationship, and I noticed him. He is just plain gorgeous. You need to talk to him the next time you see him."

"He may look like Sam Elliot, but I don't know him, and I really can't picture him in my world. Although he looked a little better this time, he is just too grubby around the edges. He probably hasn't read a book in years. And you are wrong; I have been paying attention to men who show an interest. I had coffee with the manager of the Fred Meyer store this last week. He even rides, but he has been married three times. I'm not looking for a husband, but that kind of scares me."

I quickly fill the guys in on how I met the manager and about our coffee date. I hate to actually call it a date. I'm not ready to date anyone.

"Tell you what. You may not be ready for a super long ride on your scooter, but you and I could take my bike over to Wenatchee this next month. They have a charity ride called, "Run for the Border" and it goes from Wenatchee to just before the Canadian border. I know a number of bikers who join that one. I can introduce you to some great people."

"Do I need to be gay to join in?" I can't resist the tease or the smile I give him. "Or are you trying to play matchmaker?" as I consider the reaction from my daughter and my friends.

Larry laughs. "No, you don't need to be gay, and I honestly don't think you'll need a matchmaker when you are ready. I'm not sure if any of them even know I'm gay since Ed doesn't ever ride with me, not that I try to keep that a secret. It never comes up. It will just be fun. They are a nice group of people. Think about it."

I keep the ride in Wenatchee in the back of my mind over the next few weeks. I like taking advantage of the highways in this area of South King County. There are three main highways between Seattle to the north of Federal Way and Tacoma to the south. Historic Highway 99 runs from Canada through Washington and Oregon to California, although like Route 66 there are a number of breaks along the way. It is generally a west side passage through the heart of the cities it connects. I have yet to ride it from my house in the southwest section of Federal Way to my office in the older section. But I have ridden around town on other short trips. Federal Way has no historic downtown area like its neighbors. It was a series of strip malls that organized as a city in the mid-1970s. Here Highway 99 is more basic city street than highway with lots of stoplights. For a motorcycle rider, those stoplights mean stopping behind a line without tipping the bike over. This is why I spent so many hours of practice in that parking lot. Being able to ride in the parking lot has helped me gain confidence on my bike. Soon I'll be ready to tackle those Highway 99 stoplights.

Highway 167 lies in the river valley to the east, forming a path from Mt. Rainer to the Puget Sound. The roadway connects to highways going farther east and other parts of Washington State. Federal Way lies on a ridge between Puget Sound to the west and the river valley to the east. I finally feel brave enough to ride my bike down the hill and onto Highway 167 to join my friends on our walk in Kent. I often make a loop by selecting a different road to climb back up the hill. The highways and streets from river to Sound all climb that ridge. I selected the 650, so I could make that climb easily. I had the power I needed when Larry and I had lunch at Salty's. I am not quite ready to tackle the speeds on Interstate 5, which occupies the middle ground from Canada through California, but I am relaxing into my expanded rides. I truly enjoy the sights, sounds, and smells that I can only experience on a bike. I try very hard not to think about the rides Jim and I had made in the short time we had the Goldwing. I need to focus on my life now. There is no way to go back.

Chapter Seventeen

Claire dances into my office in the early morning a few days later shaking a file. Annie, my escrow assistant, is right behind her, doubled over in laughter. "I have the one. The perfect one, and just for you," she sings off tune to music only she can hear.

"Oh, does this mean you have met your transaction goal for this month if we get this one closed?"

With a pirouette, she lays the file on my desk giggling. "Nope. This is the man for you. He is single after a non-messy divorce about four years ago, is employed as a lawyer in a good firm downtown, and is closing on a beautiful house down near the water on Redondo Beach with enough money left over to buy new furniture for the whole house if he wants." She takes a deep breath before she goes on. "On top of all of that, he is movie star gorgeous in a George Hamilton way. Is George Hamilton still alive? Anyway, Andrew is at least six feet tall and slim with deep blue eyes and dark hair with just a touch of silver at the temples. Why do men always look so debonair with silver hair that way? I don't know if he has a cute butt because he had on a suit when I met him, but I'll bet he does. I know that once you meet him, you'd let him eat crackers in your bed anytime!" Still dancing, she comes around my desk to give me a hug before she dances towards the door.

By now, I am laughing as hard as Annie. "So, Annie, did you see him too? Is she crazier than normal, or is he this good-looking?"

"Well, I only talked to him for a minute or two when he dropped off forms to help clear title on that house, but he is good-looking. I really liked his voice. It was deep and rich sounding. I thought movie star but couldn't decide on which one. George Hamilton always seemed too much like a snake oil salesman, but Mr. Simmons seems more real, sincere maybe. Claire is right, though, about the cracker crumbs."

"If he is this good-looking and single, he is probably gay or a control freak. Besides, as I've told both of you, I am just not ready to jump into dating. I'm a one-man woman, and I've had my one man. I'm okay with that. Now, both of you go back to work. I have papers to get ready for a signing this afternoon. I'll worry about Mr. Simmons when it is his turn. Claire, do you think you will be normal enough to be seen in public by lunchtime? I'd really like Mexican food."

"Mexican it will be, and I try to live my life after your model; normal is always negotiable."

The morning passes quickly. Over lunch, we catch up on Claire's difficulties with her husband and rehash my coffee date. I still haven't decided to accept his invitation for a ride and dinner. She really thinks I should give the poor man a second chance, but I'm just not sure. "He is nice, but I think once was enough. I really don't know where this might go. I only want a friend. Dinner may head us in the wrong direction. I honestly don't know what he wants."

"Hopefully, you didn't spend all of your time talking about Jim. That can be a real turn off. Focus on your here and now not your history. Learning to ride is something new and exciting for you. Go with it. I've never met a man yet who doesn't dream about motorcycles. "

Two days later, it is my turn to dance into the office. Both Annie and Claire hug their coffee cups and look at me like I've lost my mind. Claire almost shouts, "Maggie, you had sex with that store manager! Good for you."

That stops me in my tracks. "No! See, I'm wearing my riding gear? I rode my scooter to work for the first time. Didn't I tell you I wasn't interested in the store manager?"

Claire gives a big sigh as she leads Annie out to see my bike. I head to the ladies' room to make myself more presentable for a busy day. The famous Mr. Simmons will be coming in this morning to sign his closing papers. I'm betting that he is not as cute as the women have stated, but even if he is, I'm not looking for a man.

Two hours later, I have to concede that Claire and Annie are correct. Andrew Simmons is movie star gorgeous and his suit looks like it was molded to his body. Flashes of Sam Elliot come to mind, but I push them aside. I really need to focus on my job. "Mr. Simmons, I'm Maggie King," as we shake hands. I make note that he has a firm but not crushing grip. I swear a shot of electricity jumps up my arm. "Please have a seat, and let's get started. Annie said you exercised your option to pick up your copies yesterday so this should go quickly. When we finish, please let Annie know if you'd like to have a new set of copies showing signatures."

With only a brief hesitation, he replies, "Please, Mrs. King, call me Andrew, and a second set of papers won't be necessary. Have we met before?"

Oh gosh, the voice does match that good-looking body. His voice sounds a bit familiar, but it is probably from an actor. Of course, he is an attorney so his voice is as essential to his career as it would be to an actor, and many attorneys know how to play a role when they are in court. At least that is the way TV shows portray them. I don't normally have an attorney as a client. They usually use another attorney as an escrow agent. "Okay, Andrew, I'm Maggie, and I think I'd remember if we've met before. Here is your pen, and we'll get started."

The signing goes quickly, but it is only a small part of my job. I'll spend another two to three hours notarizing and reviewing every page for proper dates, initials, and signatures. I'm still amazed that my math degree brought me into escrow. I can balance charges, but have never considered myself a detail person. Andrew interrupts my feeble attempts to direct my mind back to my job.

"Now that we have finished this, will you let me take you to lunch?"

"That is very sweet, but I still have lots of work to do and another signing shortly. In addition, I don't think that lunch is appropriate with a client. I'm sure you understand."

"After this is recorded, I will no longer be a client, so I'll take that as a raincheck. Have a good day, Maggie."

Seconds after he goes out the door, Claire and Annie pop their heads into my office. "Did I lie to you? Doesn't he make you want to drop to your knees and bury your head between his legs? If I weren't married, I'd jump his bones in a second."

"Speak for yourself, Claire. I'm also married, and I'd jump his bones no matter what, but he didn't give me a second look. Did you really turn down his offer for lunch? What are you thinking, girl?" Annie asks with a frown on her face.

"I'm thinking I have work to do. Besides, I rode the bike, so I'm not going anywhere for lunch. There is no way I'm getting into a car with a perfect stranger."

"Perfect he is, but he is no stranger. Remember. I've seen his bank statements, credit report, and employment history. You would never get that type of information on a stranger. Next time he asks, say YES!"

I can almost feel Claire's feet in the middle of my back as I settle in to finish my day. He is good-looking, but I am not shopping for a man. He is a client.

Late the next day, the Simmons file is closed and settled when I call the sellers and real estate agents to let them know their checks are ready. I also call Andrew to tell him he may pick up his keys from the agent. I try to do this for every client giving each a personal touch. Listening to Andrew's voice does make it seem more than worth the effort. I really wish all of our clients were as nice. He again asks me to lunch, but again, I decline. His invitation does give me very pleasant thoughts as I change from my suit and heels back into my riding gear. I've agreed to join Mike for a trip to Maple Valley where he promises the best BBQ I've ever eaten. I keep repeating to myself that by riding my own bike, this is not a date.

Chapter Eighteen

Mike smiles as I walk out of my office. He is leaning against a very old Kawasaki. He had not lied when he told me that it didn't look as good as my bike. The black paint shows a number of rust spots and the chrome doesn't shine but gives off more of a dull glow that almost matches the gray of my bike. Wow, I need to think of something good to say about his bike. Even his leathers look as old as his bike. "Hi, Mike. Your bike really is vintage. I bet it could tell some tales."

"I've ridden it for almost thirty years now, so the bike and I have shared a lot of miles. I've often thought about getting something newer and more powerful like a Harley, but I just can't bear the thought of selling her. She may not look great, but she runs like a top. Are you ready to head out? You can follow me. I'll watch that I don't lose you at a stoplight or turn along the way."

"I'm ready." Once I pull my helmet down, I will no longer be able to hear him. *It was so easy on the Goldwing with Jim. We had those headsets in our helmets. Time to let go of Jim and the Goldwing. Focus on this ride and on Mike. You are allowed to have fun.*

Mike leads a direct path through Federal Way and then down the hill on the Peasley Canyon road. I concentrate on the curves in the Canyon. It is hard not to look for the wonderful spring flowers that I know cover the Canyon walls. Maybe this next weekend I'll come this way and stop so I can look for the trillium and Dutchman britches I love to find each spring. Mike turns onto the Highway 18 and 167 interchange. He had told me we would take Highway 18 past Auburn and Kent to Maple Valley. It can be a busy road during the evening commute.

I'm still a little uncomfortable with merging traffic. Drivers just don't pay attention to motorcycles. Once we are on Highway 18, I relax a bit for the trip to the Maple Valley turn off that we need. I even remember to give the Biker's Salute to the bikers coming at us. I'm not yet ready to totally take my left hand off the handlebars so they may not have seen my raised fingers. I'll need to practice that so I don't look like a total dork, or even worse make a sudden unsteady swerve.

The exit is a gentle curve with a straight section before the stop sign. As we turn onto the side street, I can see the BBQ sign just ahead on the right. That means I'll need to make a left turn across traffic when we leave. I'm still a little hesitant about turning in front of any oncoming traffic. I know my bike has the power, but I need to know I can stay in control. Oh well, I'll mention that to Mike when we are ready to go. Now I'm ready to eat. I am surprised by the number of bikes lined up in front as we park ours. Most of those bikes are Harleys. I hope no one teases me about my scooter.

We discuss the menu options shown on the chalkboard as we stand in the line to order our food. It smells so delicious; I have a hard time making my selections. Mike tells me that he has tried the homemade specialty potato salad and the coleslaw and all of the BBQ meats, and it's impossible to go wrong with any of them. He also adds that both the potato salad and the coleslaw are homemade specialties. After placing our orders, Mike insists on paying for both dinners, so I guess this really is a date.

Taking our drinks outside, Mike says, "Whenever possible, bikers like to be near their bikes. There is no way we could stop it if someone knocked one over, but at least we could see who did it."

"I don't mind if people look as long as they don't touch," says a man from an adjacent table. I turn to look at him. He has a long snow-white beard and hair hanging below his do-rag. His face has wrinkles to complement his white hair. He frowns at me as he says, "So are you the little lady who is riding that sissy scooter?"

Before I could answer, the large woman sitting beside him gives him a slap on his bare arm. "Don't you be giving her any shit, Old Man. Remember that you had to trade off your old Harley for your three-wheeler. It is still a Harley, but it is not one of the big boy bikes anymore. She is riding on her own, so give her some respect." He just grumbles as his friends at the table all chuckle.

She swings her legs over the bench at the picnic table so she is facing me. "I saw you ride in. How do you like your scooter? I have been thinking I might go that route rather than trading my Harley for a three-wheeler. At seventy, it is just getting too hard to mount my bike. It will still be a few minutes before our food is ready. Can you and I go look at your scooter?"

Wow! A Harley rider who wants to know about my Bergman is a surprise. I give her a nod as I get to my feet. Mike gives me a big smile. "I'm Maggie, and I'd love to show you my scooter." I know enough to not call the Bergman a 'bike' with this group. Some Harley riders would even object if Mike called his Kawasaki a motorcycle.

She and I walk over to the Bergman as she says, "I'm Lou. Let me tell you getting old is really hard for bikers. Some of us just don't want to accept that our lives need to change. Zed, there needed to crash his Soft-tail before he went for the 3-wheeler. He thought I was nuts when I mentioned a scooter. So how big is the engine in this baby? How long have you been riding it?"

I fill her in on the details as she sits on the bike. I hand her the keys so she can fire it up. I hope she doesn't decide to take it for a ride! "Well, it doesn't sound like the roar of my Harley, but it doesn't sound like a lawnmower either. This looks like it would be fun to ride. Thanks. By the way, I love your 'Red Hat Society' helmet. I should consider getting a red one as well." She hands back my keys, and I realize that I had been holding my breath.

Mike calls out, "Our dinner is here." Lou and I return to the tables where she quickly digs into her BBQ sandwich. I try to listen to Mike talk about things at the store rather than eavesdrop on the discussion about bikes at Lou's table. Zed still didn't think she should even consider a scooter. I have the feeling that she will do whatever she wants rather than what he thinks.

Mike and I talk about the ride home as it starts to get dark. I've never ridden in the dark before, but I know the route well once we leave the BBQ parking lot. He understands my concerns about that first left. Luckily it is just twilight, so visibility isn't an extreme issue. I just hate knowing that some cars don't turn on their headlights until it is fully dark. We agree to go our separate ways once we get off Highway 18 in South Federal Way. I'm relieved that Mike agrees to not see me all the way to my house. This may have been a real date, but I'm not ready to deal with turning him away at my door. I do know that inviting him in could lead to expectations of more. I'm truly not ready for 'more'. I'm not sure that I'm even ready to have a serious date with anyone. Tonight has been fun, but this step is enough.

Chapter Nineteen

Shortly after I settle into my office the following morning, Annie comes in and closes the door. "Mr. Simmons is here and asked to see you for just a couple of minutes. You don't have any appointments this morning, so can I show him in?"

Doesn't the man give up? Claire and Denise both said I need to say yes if he asks again. I'm still not sure I'm ready, but there is no time like the present. Taking a deep breath, I blurt out, "Okay."

As Annie heads out, and Andrew walks in, I can hear Claire giggling at Annie's desk. Andrew has a dozen pink roses in his hand. "Think of these as both a thank you for getting the house closed so quickly, and a bribe to see if you will finally go to lunch with me. Is it working?" He gives me a big smile as he raises one eyebrow.

I'm afraid Annie and Claire will start jumping up and down, but I have decided to say yes to lunch. How can any woman turn down an offer like this? We agree to meet at Verrazano's Italian Restaurant in Federal Way. It has great food and a breathtaking view of the Puget Sound from the bluff. Best of all, today I'm driving my car rather than riding the bike.

As soon as he walks out the door, Claire enters my office. She's dying to explain to me what the colors symbolize from the dozen yellow roses Andrew gave her and the single white one he brought Annie. But she quickly moves on after I tell her I agreed to have lunch with him. Yelling at Annie, she asks, "Does Maggie have appointments this afternoon? If so, you may need to cancel them if she decides to have sex with Andrew after their lunch."

"I did not say anything about having sex with Andrew! We are having lunch at Verrazano's, not the No Tell Motel. Think of something other than me having sex. Now, out of my office. I don't want to discuss this here. We can talk tonight while we walk."

I do not want to let Claire or Annie know that I have butterflies in my stomach. Andrew is definitely not Mike Smith, the store manager. Despite the suit and tie, Andrew gives off an air of testosterone. I haven't decided if it is a good thing or a bad one, but it has my interest.

Lunch by Claire's standards is tame. The Italian food is wonderful. We chat about the view of the Sound, work, college days, and family. He says that he and his ex-wife have one son who lives and works in New York. I tell him about Sharon and Richard and make a very concentrated effort to not mention Jim. The ladies are right; telling a man all about the love of my life is not a great way to get to know him. Andrew seems like a nice man who might be fun to be with to see a movie or to dinner. I find that it is easy to just relax and enjoy myself. If he asks again, I know I will say yes.

I tell Claire and Annie that lunch was just lunch and there is nothing to discuss. During our after-work walk, the ladies want details about Andrew. As I do just that, I realize that I still don't know that much about the man. He is very good at answering questions by asking questions without providing much information about himself. That is a talent I wish I had. When I announce to the group that I had not talked about Jim or even mentioned his name, they declare that they would buy my glass of wine tonight. They say I'm making progress, and they can't wait until I see him again. There are those feet in the middle of my back once more, but I don't think I mind. I try not to think about this as taking baby steps. I'm just living my life.

Thursday is a rainy day, so I do not ride the bike. Andrew calls to ask if I like seafood. When I tell him yes, he suggests that he pick me up for lunch at McGraths. We agree on an early lunch but that I'll meet him there. I still feel much more confident, knowing I can leave anytime if I feel uncomfortable. I don't intend to tell Claire or Annie about lunch. I'm going because I want to, not because they are pushing. Somehow, that seems important.

This time over lunch, I try to answer Andrew's questions with questions of my own. Neither of us provides any additional personal information. Instead, we move on to chatting about our favorite foods and restaurants. Federal Way is about halfway between Seattle and Tacoma. There are almost 200 restaurants in the area. That gives us a lot to talk about. Lunch goes almost too fast.

Andrew walks me to my car, but before I can get in, he takes my face in his hands and kisses me. It isn't a curl my toes, spread my legs kind of kiss, but it is a very nice kiss. Remembering Jim's kisses, I draw in slow breaths. *Change your thoughts now Maggie. Jim doesn't belong here.* Giving Andrew my full attention, I smile as he says, "How about dinner tomorrow night at Salty's? I think you mentioned that you liked it, and there are more dinner selections on the menu there than here at McGrath's. Can I pick you up?"

Before I can give it any serious thought, I quickly agree once again but insist on meeting him there. "Keep this up, Maggie, and I'm going to think you don't trust me." Giving me a light kiss, he holds my car door open.

My head is spinning as I drive back to the office. *What have I gotten myself into? This is going too fast, and the ladies will not be any help. Maybe I need to tell Sharon all about it, so someone tells me to cancel this dinner. Oh no, that would be more like telling my mother. She never liked anyone or anything. I am strong, and it is just dinner. I can do this.*

Chapter Twenty

I decide to tell Ed and Larry about my dinner plans. I am just meeting the man at a restaurant. The restaurant is a very public place, but the parking lot is a bit dark at the edges. It just seems smarter to let someone know where I'll be and with whom. I really don't want to tell Claire, Megan, or Denise. I'm nervous enough without them making more out of this than just dinner. At some point, I may need to tell my children that I have decided to date but not yet. It isn't like I have actually started a relationship with Andrew or Mike. This is just dinner.

After spending forty-five minutes pulling things out of my closet and putting them back, I call Ed. I need some fashion help, and he is my go-to man for that. I usually wear suits to work and jeans at home. I want something more feminine. I think I want a dress but nothing too sexy. I remember I had a group of outfits that I called date dresses when Jim and I first met. I updated those a few years back for special evenings out, but they just don't seem right. Ed actually owns a dress shop and has wonderful ideas on how to work with what I already have. Best of all, he is right next door and can't wait to help.

"Let's see what you have. You know it has been far too long since you invited me to work with your closet. This is really something we should do at least twice a year. You have an excellent figure for a woman your age, and that silver hair just glows, so we need to play those things up. You are right about those dresses. They were nice but just not right for the new Maggie."

"Now remember I'm not looking for sexy. I want a look that is comfortable, not too casual and not too much like my business suits."

"You really need to come to the shop soon, so we have a few more options, but I think I have some things here to get us started. You just have to trust me, Maggie. Have I ever let you down? Now, what do you think of either this blouse and this skirt or this other combination?" He drapes first one and then another of the outfits across his arm with a cock of his head and a bit of a twirl. He can be so dramatic. I can't help laughing.

"Don't I have something in basic black?" I ask with a frown. "Don't I have a little black dress like every woman should have? Emerald green and navy blue are not black. Didn't you tell me to never wear that blue blouse with that blue suit? You did say I could wear the green skirt with its matching blouse, but we always added a black jacket. Am I wearing a suit jacket tonight? How is that any different from a plain suit? Ed, you are here to help me." I try to keep the panic out of my voice.

"I am helping you. Either the green or the blue will look wonderful with that scarf I gave you for Christmas. You can wear it like a shawl if you are cool. The short sleeves look very feminine, and with the top two buttons undone you can hint at sexy without being too much for your comfort zone. You can add a simple pendant, so he has something to comment on if he stares at your breasts. And both of those skirts fit just right to show off your curves. You lost weight last year, but I think you have added muscle from your walks, so you are looking very shapely. You will be comfortable because everything fits like it was made just for you. Pick one and try it on. You will see that I'm right."

Trying the green, with the scarf, I must admit that Ed is right. I already knew that the malachite pendant went well with the blouse. *Why didn't I think of this? More importantly, why is this so important? This is just dinner with a man who may become a friend.*

I swear Ed can read my mind. "You look fabulous. That is such a nice color on you. Your silver hair provides sparkle, and the green sets off your very blue eyes. What time is your date? Do I get to meet him? Oh, and one more thing; it is much easier for a woman to take off a skirt and blouse than it is to slide out of a dress. When we update your wardrobe, I'll insist that there be no back zippers for you. They make it just too hard for you to strip." I am torn between wanting to hit the man or start laughing. Laughter wins.

Chapter Twenty-One

Ed did nothing to settle my nerves before I drive down the hill to Salty's. No matter how I try to spin it, this is actually a date. BBQ dinner with Mike was a bike ride. This is a date with a handsome man. I arrive at Salty's faster than I really want. I'm not sure I'm prepared because I don't know what to expect. I haven't had a dinner date in almost thirty years. *Oh, Jim, I miss you so much.*

Andrew is waiting for me outside the front door. He gives me a quick hug as we greet, and I take a deep breath as I repeat my mantra to myself, *I can do this. It will be okay. I am a strong independent woman.* I honestly hope I remember to smile. This is supposed to be fun. He takes my hand after opening the door and leads me to a window seat. As always, the view gives me pause. The water has taken on a golden tone as the sun sets.

I think Andrew realizes that I'm nervous, as he tells a funny story about something that happened in court today. I would never have thought of King County Court as a funny place, but he manages to make it appear that way. It is clear, he likes what he does. Placing our orders, we continue the light banter as I sip a glass of wine. *This is easy. Why was I so worried? I can handle this dating stuff, kind of like riding a bike.*

I relax even more with the second glass of wine over dinner. I usually try to stick to one glass when I'm driving, but it really goes well with the spicy fish highlighted as the evening's special. I don't even remember when Andrew ordered the second glass, but I know that he must have. We pass on dessert, and Andrew suggests a walk on the Redondo Beach pier. As soon as we reach the end of the pier, I catch my heel in the space between the planks, and I would have fallen if Andrew hadn't put his arm around me at that very moment.

Instead of falling on my nose, I fall against him. I laugh as he pushes my hair out of my eyes as he cups my face. Then he kisses me, and the last thing I think about is hair in my eyes. He really knows how to kiss a woman. One kiss leads to another, and then he is holding me close as he covers my face and neck with kisses. My head spins once again. I love the way my body feels molded against his. When he says, "My house is only a few blocks away. Let's go there for a nightcap." I can only nod my head. I don't trust my voice for fear, I'll shout out, "Yes!" scaring the sea birds.

Taking off my shoes, I walk barefoot to the car, so I don't have to worry about catching my heel again. Once I reach my car, I slide back on my shoes, and concentrate on following Andrew's car as he heads to the next street up. As I pull into the driveway, I realize that Claire was correct. The house is beautiful. Andrew opens my car door and kisses me before leading the way to his front door. "I'm sorry that the place is a mess. Most of the furniture has not yet arrived, and I'm still unpacking."

I barely have time to look around before he kisses me again. He finds a place on my neck that has me curling my toes. I kick off my shoes and stand on my tiptoes as I pull him closer. The only conscious thought I have is to remember to breathe. This is what I want, and this is just what I need now. Nothing else matters. Unbuttoning my blouse, he buries his face in my breasts. Without a word, he scoops me into his arms and carries me into the bedroom. He stands me beside the bed as he pushes my blouse from my shoulders. I fumble with the buttons on his shirt as he unzips my skirt. I pull his shirt from his pants and kiss his shoulder as he unhooks my bra. He trails kisses down my stomach as he rolls my panties down. Megan was right when she said that a smart woman never wears pantyhose on a date. There is no way to remove them gracefully. All I can think about is how wonderful I feel as the heat spreads through my body. His fingers slide into me, and an orgasm slams me instantly. "Oh, God." Every part of my body is on fire.

Andrew eases me onto the bed and sheds his pants and shorts before joining me. He doesn't need to say a word. Every inch of the man is gorgeous. I'm not sure I've ever considered a penis as a work of art, but I'm sure his qualifies. I start to kiss my way down his body, but he pulls me up and drops down to quickly cover my core with his mouth. He uses teeth and tongue to bring me to one orgasm after another. I can do nothing but moan with passion. I think I am going to die from pleasure when he slowly slides into me and then pauses. I contract around him. My body responds as he starts a gentle rocking that quickly builds to a burning need in both of us. I try to hold back but feel like shattered glass when I explode in orgasm one final time. I feel Andrew follow me over that cliff. I wait for the world to stop spinning and for my breath to come back. He cradles me in his arms and kisses the top of my head. He holds me gently as we float. The world slowly settles back into place.

We must have fallen asleep because I woke with a start. I have rolled to my side with my back to him in a spoon position. His arm and leg are draped across me. His breath comes across my shoulder with just a light snore. My mind moves from peace to panic in a flash. I slide out of bed, picking up my clothes as I head into the bathroom. *Oh my God, I had sex with a stranger.* Andrew is waiting for me when I step out fully dressed. "Where are you going, Maggie?"

"I have to go home. My children like to drop in on Saturday morning for coffee. I also have my friend's dog, and he needs to be let out. I really need to be there."

"It's early yet, come back to bed. You feel so good beside me."

I put on my shoes and pick up my keys. "Sounds wonderful, but I really need to go." I give him a quick kiss and almost run for the door.

As I drive home, I can't tell my mother's voice in my head from my own. *What was I thinking? I don't know him, and I don't want to just have sex with a man I don't love. Was it the wine? I'm a slut. I know I can't drink two glasses of wine without feeling it. I am not some twenty-year-old slut who will spread her legs for the first man who kisses her. I can't do this. I can't see him again. No, no, no! What if my children find out? How can I face them? They don't know, and they don't need to know. You never need to see him again, and things will be just fine.*

My house seems to be miles away. I'll get to my own house with my cat, and everything will be okay. It will be okay. I keep telling myself that as I crawl into my own bed.

Chapter Twenty-Two

Saturday morning dawns bright and sunny after the rain on Friday. I wake feeling not quite so sunny. Murphy Jones, the cat is sitting on my chest with his nose pressed against mine. I instantly compare his "kisses" to the way Andrew kissed me. Was last night wonderful or a huge mistake? I really don't know how the world works for mature single women. I do know that I have to get my mother out of my head. We didn't agree on anything when I was younger, so I really don't need her advice now. I need to call the ladies. A fast early morning walk with their input should help put my world right again. I make the calls.

When we meet an hour later, Megan is still sipping her Starbucks coffee. She had gotten in on a late flight. I brought her dog, Muffin so he can walk with us and go home with her. Denise had stopped to drop her son with her parents. At eleven years old, he did not like the early morning wakeup call but loves the way Grandma cooks a big breakfast, and Grandpa is always working on a project where his help is needed. He is a great kid, but our walks are not the right place for him most of the time. Who knew that fifty-year-old women could be so graphic at times?

Claire has worry lines on her face as she kicks things off. "Okay, Miss Maggie. What is wrong? I thought you had a first date with Andrew last night. Was it awful? Does he talk with food in his mouth? Or pick his nose at the table? What?"

Megan brightens up, "You had an actual date with Andrew, the attorney? What could be so wrong with that? You had said he was handsome and funny."

Denise chimes in, "I'll bet you slept with him. Is that it?"

The group stops short and turns to look at me. I squeak out, "Yes."

"Yes, to what? Did you actually sleep with him?"

"Oh, you wild woman, you. How was it? Why are you upset? It is not like you've never had sex before."

By now, I am almost in tears. "It was wonderful. He was so gentle and seemed to know just what I like and needed. I thought my heart was going to stop. Maybe it was the two glasses of wine. But then later, I woke with my mother's voice in my head calling me a slut like she did when I was a teenager. I don't know how to be a single woman dating at this age. I'm not sure I was ever a wild woman. I just know that even if I acted like a slut, I need to get my mother out of my head."

Megan pulls me into a hug as she quietly whispers in my ear, "I knew your mother most of my life. She was a fake person who smiled at strangers and said terrible things to you. She has been gone for six years, and that, my dear, is a good thing. She tried to destroy your relationship with Jim from the day you met him. You didn't let her win. Don't let her destroy this. And you could never be a slut no matter how many men you decide to sleep with."

Now I am in tears. Denise loops her arm through mine and starts to pull me back into our walk. "Okay, girlfriend, let's go over the dating rules. Number one—The only way you could be a slut is if you got paid for it and didn't actually like it. Number two—It is okay to have sex with a man when you feel like it. Number three—Watch out for wine on a first date. In fact, watch your glass at all times. The sex needs to be your idea, not some chemical added to your glass. And Number four—Go to the drug store and buy a big box of condoms. Make sure he always wears protection."

"I always keep condoms in my purse. Who knows when you will meet a man who knows how to press those buttons? Remember at this age, it is not about saying 'No' but remembering to say 'Yes' in the limited time we have left," Megan states with a big smile on her face.

"Oh, I need to remember to come back to that, Megan," Claire says. "I'm sure the smile says there is a great story there, but for now, Maggie, give us more details about the sex, and Denise is right about the rules. Safety first, and let the good times roll. Gone are the days when you would claim that doing it in a car didn't count; that it was just an oops. Now there is nothing wrong with enjoying sex. That is the only reason that I've stayed married to my husband. The man is a jerk, but the sex is good, and I don't have to go through that dating routine to get it. Now back to those details."

It is amazing how my friends can help me remember to breathe and to smile. Megan's words have helped quiet my mother's voice. It is much too easy to hear her lectures all over again. I feel sorry for Mother; she must have been so unhappy with her life.

"I don't intend to give you many more details, but when we walked out on the Redondo pier, and he started kissing me, my toes curled."

"You are just lucky that the pier didn't smell like fish. If the squid are gathered there, the place is packed."

"I still want details!"

"Is the rest of him as gorgeous as the parts I saw?"

The world is back to normal, and our walking and talking continue. I, however, don't tell them just how gorgeous all parts of the man are. That is for me to keep close.

Chapter Twenty-Three

Back home, I shower and then check out the Destination Harley website. They are having a Ladies Ride from Tacoma to Silverdale. Silverdale is hosting a taco salad ladies' lunch, and Tacoma will offer BBQ hamburgers for the guys. It is time to try a group ride. I know a lot of the women will be on smaller Harleys or Kawasakis, but there may be another scooter rider or two. I doubt the women will make bad jokes like some of the men I've met. I still remember the sneer on our Harley Man's face.

I will need to ride on Interstate 5 for part of this trip. Although the roadway can be complete gridlock in early mornings or afternoons during the week, most weekends the traffic moves at or above the posted Interstate speed limit of 60 in this area. Today will be the first time I will merge and ride at that speed. This is the second reason I wanted the power of the 650. I feel almost like a sixteen-year-old with a new driver's license. I may know the roadway well, but it will present new perils on my bike. The route the group ride will take to and from Silverdale crosses both the new and old Tacoma Narrows Bridges over a section of Puget Sound. I remember from the rides Jim and I had taken that bridges may have metal mesh roadbeds. These can make it harder to steer any bike but especially one with smaller tires. A small Vespa could not be ridden on the Interstate, nor manage the bridge deck. For all of this, I have my big girl bike.

There are ten or twelve women grouped around as many bikes when I arrive at Destination's parking lot. I had allowed forty-five minutes to make the ten-minute trip but realize things start earlier than I had expected for this type of event. I am just glad that traffic was light and the ride was uneventful. The sales clerk from the riding gear department has a clipboard and gives me a big smile as I park my bike. "We didn't actually meet when you and your friends were in before, but I remember you. You and your friends were having so much fun, that you made my day. I'm Nicole, and I'll be leading this ride. Welcome, is this your first group ride?"

"It is. Does it show?"

"Oh no, I just hadn't seen you on a ride before. I have an information card for you to complete. This will also add you to our mailing list about future rides. We do have a five-dollar charge for lunch. All of that goes to Children's Hospital. We try to rotate donations to different charities for our rides. We think everyone wins that way."

"Here is the five dollars, and let's match it for a total of ten. They do good work. What happens next?"

"We will go over communication for on the road, and will then head out five minutes after the hour. We won't make any stops along the way unless there is an emergency. You might want to beat the last-minute rush to the ladies' room if you need. Pour yourself some coffee and introduce yourself. Most of these women have ridden together before."

I quickly complete the card. I do have to walk to the back of my bike to read my plate number. Just as I finish, a slim older woman walks over and puts out her hand to shake mine. She is holding a red helmet in her other hand. "I'm Sue. It is nice to see a woman with a little silver in her hair joining us. I'm sixty-eight, and that is my red trike. I really like the looks of your scooter. Is it fast?"

A trike requires different riding skills than a bike. Although it is said they are not hard to learn to ride, it is easier if you've never learned to ride a motorcycle. Both Harleys and Goldwings are popular bikes for trike conversions, and they share one common feature. For both, the finished trike costs almost two times the original price of the bike. She has earned my admiration. In addition, Sue has reassured me that I'm not too old for this riding business.

"Sue, I'm Maggie, and that is a beautiful Harley. I had hoped for a red bike, but settled for gray. The red on yours is perfect."

"Well, thanks. With a trike conversion, you get to pick your color just like your helmet. At least all of these young things will recognize us for our red helmets. Nice choice. So, tell me about your scooter. I've seen them around, but never met anyone who has actually ridden one."

The younger women join us as we talk bikes, and I fill them in on the scooter. As I had guessed, they were supportive rather than critical of my choice. This should be a fun day and a wonderful way to not think about Andrew. Nicole runs through the guidelines for riding as a group. I notice that some of the women have blue tooth headsets on their helmets. They make the adjustments needed to be on the same channel. If I do many of these rides, I might want to add that. It could be hard for women to be together for a forty-five to sixty-minute ride in silence! I'm sure some of the gals also ride with their husbands or boyfriends, and a headset makes riding more fun. For the rest of us, Nicole will use some hand signals that will be passed down the line as needed. She suggests that I stay in the middle of the group so someone can let her know if I have trouble. The sound of twelve bikes starting up almost at once takes me by surprise. Compared to the Harleys in the group, I'm sure mine sounds more like an electric lawn mower. Women may not be impressed with the sound, but the men on the other side of the parking lot turn to watch as we pull out.

The highway loops around the edges of Tacoma before crossing the Tacoma Narrows. The bridge is high, and the view of the Sound to both north and south is always spectacular. I am too nervous to even look. Once we are across and start up the hill, I start to relax just a bit. The road is more rural until we drop down along the Sound outside of Bremerton, and then rural again until we come into Silverdale. I've always loved driving this way, and on the bike, it is fabulous. This is the Washington State most people picture–tall trees and sparkling water. I'm really glad I am doing this.

Over lunch, we trade names and swap stories. Refreshed, we are ready to make the return trip. Sue makes an announcement to the group, "I'll be riding directly behind Maggie. We are officially forming the Tacoma motorcycle riders' chapter of the Red Helmet Society. I don't want anyone to miss us." She makes me laugh. We both have to answer questions about the significance of red helmets. I've relaxed enough to enjoy more of the scenery on the return ride. There is no doubt in my mind about how much I enjoy riding. I may not be able to explain it, but it is like nothing else. I also love the comradery of the women who are riding around me. Sue and I trade contact information. We hope to do more rides together in the future. I'm starting to feel like part of the biking community. This means I will be shopping for that blue tooth headset.

Chapter Twenty-Four

Once we arrive back at Destination in Tacoma, I head for the ladies' room. It has not been a long ride, and I'm not far from home, but I really need the break. I would not want to admit to the other women that I'm getting tired. They are all laughing and joking as we form a line outside the small ladies' room. They all seem energized. I spent too much of the trip being tense. Home sounds great.

As I walk back toward my bike a few minutes later, I see that familiar Harley parked next to it. The Harley Man has removed his helmet as he chats with another rider. I stop in my tracks. Even with his back to me, I think I know him. A clean-shaved Andrew slowly turns in my direction, giving me a silly grin. "Maggie, I'm so glad you are here. Did you enjoy your ride? I realized that I only have your work number, but I don't even know if it is okay to call you at home." He reaches out to take my hand. "I wanted to tell you how much I enjoyed last night. Have I told you how cute you look on your little bike? I saw you as you ladies rode in to the lot."

I need to remind myself to close my mouth as it drops open at the sight of him. My shock turns quickly to hurt. "So, you are the mystery man on the Road King, Andrew?" I pull my hand from his. "You watched me learn to ride a motorcycle and knew it when you first walked into my office. You didn't say anything about that?" I can't keep the anger out of my voice. I feel used. "You never mentioned that you also rode a motorcycle when we talked about so many things over our lunches and dinner. Was this all some type of game for you, Andrew? Watch the little woman learn to ride, but never mention it? What other surprises were you planning for me?"

Andrew throws back his head laughing. "Well, I didn't know you when I first saw you." He chuckles as he says, "You just looked like a mature woman learning to ride on a whim. I could tell you were not a Motorcycle Momma. I just thought you were cute. Over our lunches, I thought about asking you why you decided to learn to ride, but you never brought it up. I decided your riding might have been to please someone else, so I didn't mention it either."

"My reasons for learning to ride are my own. I don't need to explain them to anyone. You, however, have ridden for many years from the looks of your well-worn leathers. You are going to be teaching the motorcycle safety class. I can't believe that you didn't tell me about it, knowing that I was learning to ride. Why did you make it a mystery?" I don't know if I want to cry or kick something in anger. "The only explanation I have is that you did want to turn this revelation into a game."

"No, it isn't a game, but you are really overreacting. I thought it would be something we could laugh about. When we first talked in your office, I didn't know you were serious about riding. And you bought a scooter rather than a real bike."

"Overreacting'? I don't think so, and my scooter is a real bike." I now feel that the urge to kick something winning over the need to cry, and I know exactly who I want to kick.

Andrew laughs once more. "No darlin', you and your scooter are cute, but that is still not a real bike. You need to take a ride on the back of my Harley, so you know what a real bike is all about."

"No, Andrew, I don't *need* to do anything with you. I am fully capable of doing my own riding without advice from a man like you!" The volume of my voice has risen with my anger. He is being so condescending and smug; everything I hate in a man. Then he makes it worse.

Andrew's laughter stops. He replies in a mocking tone, "Now you are being a typical woman. I expect better of you, Maggie"

"I don't need this." Without another word, I turn my back to him, pull my helmet on, and get on my bike. I can almost hear Andrew say something to me as I fire it up. I do not look back as I pull out of the lot. I make the turns toward the freeway and home. I take deep breaths to control my anger. I'll need to concentrate on the road, and not let my anger affect my driving. Even harder is controlling my urge to cry. I thought I was done crying over a man when Jim died.

Well, at least, I don't have to worry about how I tell my children that I am dating! I don't plan to ever see that ass again. It will be a long time before I let another man hurt me like this.

On Sunday, the ladies meet for a late afternoon walk. I'm proud that I had not felt the need to call an emergency walking meeting on Saturday evening. A long hot bath and glass of wine had eased my anger. At first, my friends don't say a thing as I tell them about my discovery that Andrew is the Harley Man we have talked about for weeks. A couple of minutes of silence are more than I can handle. The words quickly tumble out of my mouth, "None of you were there. He was just so smug and arrogant. He thought it was a joke. He knew we had met, and never said a thing, especially after the way he acted about my scooter. I just don't need a man like that in my life." I feel the anger rising once again.

"No woman needs a good-looking man with a good job who brings her flowers," Claire says with a big smile.

"You're right, Claire. Maggie doesn't need a man who rides a Harley. She has her own bike. I'm sure it gives her as much of a thrill as Andrew did Friday night," Megan adds. "Wrapping her legs around her scooter has to be better than the great sex she had with him." I can see she is trying hard to not laugh.

"Sorry, Claire and Megan. Maggie needs to learn that a man with a Harley might be a jerk, but that level of testosterone is going to show up sooner or later. If the man is as good looking as Sam Elliot, knows how to make love to a woman, and rides a Harley, you need to cut him some slack."

"I'm not so sure, and I don't need to rush into anything. I've already done that with him once. I really think I want to just step back and concentrate on living my life. Maybe I should accept Larry's invitation for that Wenatchee ride this next weekend. He is going over on Friday night to join friends, but I could drive over on Saturday morning early and then come home on Sunday. The change of scenery might be good for me. Larry said he wanted to introduce me to some people he thinks will be fun."

"That might work. Andrew will either be waiting or he won't."

"It is always good to keep a man on his toes."

"Denise, do you really think you are the best one to give advice on men? You won't even date."

"Of course I can, just like we all can when it is needed."

"Time for wine." I'm still not sure just what I want to do about Andrew. He is a jerk, even if he does know how to kiss me. It is not like I'm in love with him. My problem is I can't see myself just using him for sex. Why does dating at this age still remind me of being a teenager? Why can't it just be easier?

Chapter Twenty-Five

Andrew calls me at work on Monday. I don't take his call. Annie just shakes her head when I tell her to take a message if he calls again. He calls twice more during the week. I do not take any of the calls, nor do I return them or even read the messages. I have decided that I rushed into things with Andrew, but that I can stop it right now. I do not want a man who can think the way he acted was funny no matter what my friends have said.

Saturday morning is bright and clear as I drive over the mountains to Wenatchee. Mid May offers perfect riding weather. I would really like to take my own bike, but it is hundred and fifty miles from Federal Way to Wenatchee. The Run to the Border ride is an additional hundred and fifty miles each way. That is far more than I am ready to tackle. I'll put it on my to-do list for next year. Today it should be fun riding behind Larry. I also look forward to meeting new people who like riding motorcycles.

The parking lot at the old Food Pavilion is filled with bikes and cars. Larry had said there might be between 150 and 200 motorcyclists who join this ride. I spot him near the registration tent. We argue over which of us will pay the twenty-dollar registration fee, and I win. Like other group rides, this one rotates the sponsored charities. This year it is the Chelan-Douglas Court-Appointed Special Advocates Mentorship Program for children. I make a donation to match the registration fee. We may not live in Chelan or Douglas County, but we both want to support the program. I realize that coordinating rides and charities could be a full-time job, but I doubt that it pays very well.

Larry leads me over to a group of men clustered around some beautiful bikes. Some of the men greet Larry by name and others just nod. Larry is quick to introduce me to the men he knows, and we exchange names with the others. I acknowledge that I'll never keep every name straight.

A tall slim man with silver hair joins the group, "Forget names for the rest of these jokers. Mine is the only one you need to remember. Larry, introduce me to your beautiful lady friend."

"Maggie King, I'd like you to meet Doctor Mark Johnson. Mark is a dean at Wenatchee Valley College. Mark, Maggie is my neighbor and dear friend. I had hoped you might be here today."

"Doctor Johnson, it is nice to meet you. Have you known Larry long?"

"Please call me Mark, and may I call you Maggie? Larry and I have made this ride for the last few years. So, do you have your own bike?'

"I do, but I'll be riding with Larry this year. I may just ride myself next year."

"I really want to know more about you and hear about your bike. I hope you plan to stay for the music festival once we reach Oroville. It looks like we need to mount up. Of course, you could just join me."

Smiling, I turn to walk back to Larry's bike. He puts my things into his saddlebags. Larry and I will share his room at a hotel in Omak, so we don't have to ride all of the way back in one day. With this many riders, it would be impossible for me to find a room in either Omak or Oroville at the last minute. Ed said Larry and I can have a fun slumber party even if he couldn't join us.

We put our helmets on as the sound of more than a hundred and fifty bikes turns into a roar. Spectators have gathered around the parking lot to watch as the bikes start to file out two abreast and turn toward the bridge across the

Columbia River. We are in the middle of the group. Larry will maintain that position at least until we make the stop in Omak. There are a number of small towns along the way, but most do not provide a good stopping place for this many people. I am comfortable on the back of Larry's bike, so I don't mind the ninety-five miles as it follows first the Columbia River and then the smaller Omak River. The fruit orchards that line the road are no longer in bloom, but the views of the river are delightful. I have always enjoyed the twists and turns of this road, but on the bike, it is even better. We reach Omak two hours later, and I am ready to take the break. Larry parks near two Harley Road Kings. One looks a lot like Andrew's, but I'm sure that many of them look alike. When I return from the ladies' room, Larry is chatting with both Andrew and Mark. Andrew gives me a big smile, "Maggie, I am really happy to see you." I offer no reply as I unhook my helmet from Larry's handlebars. I want to make certain that I can keep my tone normal.

Before I can say anything, Mark jumps in. "Are you ready to ride with me now, Maggie? My Harley is much smoother than Larry's BMW."

"She could ride with me because my Road King is also smooth," Andrew says.

"I'll stick with Larry but thanks for the offers." I pull my helmet down, blocking out what any of the men have to say. All conversation is again drowned out by the roar of the bikes as they are fired up. I'm happy to have that conversation end. I have fifty miles to think about how I will avoid Andrew once we get there. I'd like to tell Larry to park as far away from Andrew as he can, but I know Larry won't be able to hear me. Both Andrew and Mark pull into the row directly behind us. This day has lost its luster very quickly.

Chapter Twenty-Six

Oroville is normally a sleepy little Washington town just before the Canadian border. There had been panic in the community a few years ago when the State wanted to close camping at Osoyoos State Park. It is a popular park on the shores of Osoyoos Lake, which continues into Canada. Today the park is packed, and the entire town has gone all out for the bikers. The blues festival will run all weekend and is a big draw from both Washington and British Columbia.

Larry finds a place to park near both the taco truck and some shade trees. Spreading a blanket under a tree to reserve our space, I watch Mark and Andrew park beside Larry. After a brief discussion, Larry heads to the taco truck, and Andrew goes for beer. Mark settles into a corner of the blanket very close to me. Larry sits on the other side of me when he returns, leaving Andrew a spot diagonally opposite. Mark, Larry, and I are starting on our tacos before Andrew gets back. "Hey, why did I get stuck with the long line?"

"The beer garden will do a great business today, but so will the taco truck. Did you notice the crowd in every restaurant in town as we came through? I'm glad we were in the middle of the group, or I'd still be in line for tacos," Larry said.

The first of the bands has assembled and starts into their opening number. I wonder how the people directly in front of the stage are able to deal with the volume. We are close enough to hear well, but can't really understand each other while they are playing. I really don't mind because I don't want to talk to Andrew. Finishing up the tacos and beer, we give Mark a thumbs-up for another round. Andrew starts to move over toward Mark's place, but I stretch out with my head on my jacket, blocking him. I don't intend to get close to him. Larry raises his eyebrow and has probably guessed that Andrew is the date I told Ed about. He hasn't asked any questions, but I know we will talk about it later tonight. Mark moves in a little closer when he sits back down. He whispers in my ear as he tells me about the current band. I make a point of smiling at him as often as I can. He is a good-looking man. I don't like to play games, but Andrew can go to hell.

During the break between the first and second bands, Larry announces that he is heading back to Omak to our hotel. "Can one of you give Maggie a ride back? I hate to cut her time here." I give him a dirty look.

The men sound like a duet, "Glad to. Don't worry about Maggie. She is safe with me."

I wonder if Larry has planned this so I'll need to decide between the men. I won't put it past him. My first instinct is to tell everyone that I can go with Larry, but maybe I can use this as an opportunity to let Andrew know I'm no longer interested in him. I give Mark a big smile, "Oh, Mark, that would be wonderful. I really would like to hear the next band. I don't really want to stay all evening, but another hour or so would be nice. Would that work for you?" The sugar tone is almost enough to make me sick. Mark seems to be eating it up.

Andrew just glares at me when Mark says, "Another couple of hours would be just fine. We can drive back to Omak, and then I could head on to Wenatchee if I want."

Larry leans over to give me a quick kiss and whispers in my ear. "Have fun with the boys." He waves as he backs his bike out. Another bike instantly takes his parking spot. Andrew has moved to Larry's place on the blanket. I'm now sandwiched between two men on either side of me. I'm very happy when the music starts up again.

I have no idea how to handle conversation with the two of them.

Two hours later, I head to the line at the ladies' room. There were three times as many men as women on the rally, but the music festival filled in the spaces with more women. Still, the men outnumber the women. I am probably not the only woman with a man on each arm. I just need to think of a way to get back to Omak with only one, and then to have him disappear without an issue.

By the time I return to Mark and Andrew, Mark has folded Larry's blanket and is placing it in his saddlebag. Putting on my best smile, I greet him. "Are we ready?"

"Are you sure you don't want to ride with me, Maggie? You know I do teach the safety classes." Andrew was twisting the throttle on his bike just enough to punctuate his words.

"Thank you, Andrew, but I'll be just fine riding with Mark." I settle behind Mark as I pull my helmet down snuggly ending the conversation. I wrap my arms around Mark's slim waist and lean close. I swear the man has extra loud exhaust pipes on his bike as we roar out of the parking lot. I can see Andrew pull out right behind us. This type of double date really needs to end.

The ride from Oroville to Omak is uneventful if not peaceful. The sun has dropped in the sky but not yet set. There is a soft glow reflected off the Omak River as we ride beside it. Mark's Harley is so loud that we could not have talked if I had tried. I point to direct him to the hotel parking lot. He shuts down the bike and removes his helmet as I dismount and remove mine. He also dismounts and moves around the bike to stand very close to me. *Does he think he is coming in?* "Thank you, Mark. I really enjoyed today. You are a fun guy." *Where did Andrew go? He had been right behind us. Did he follow us into the parking lot?*

Mark pulls the blanket from the saddlebag and places it on the seat. As I reach out to pick it up, he pulls me into his arms and kisses me. I try to step back as he kisses me again as he uses both hands to grab my butt. *Wow! I need to get this under control.* I put both hands on his chest to push him back.

"We don't really have to have today end, Maggie. I could come in for a while."

"Larry is waiting for me, but thanks again for the ride."

"You could tell him you have decided to ride on to Wenatchee with me. It is still early. We could grill some steaks at my house. You could spend the night before going back to Seattle."

"Mark, you are just a little too fast for me. I'll call it a night. Thanks for the ride." I pull back and put my helmet over my chest as well as the blanket. I take two more steps back. "Have a good ride."

"You can't blame a man for trying. May I call you? I do get to the big city regularly."

"That would be fine. Good-bye." I don't want to move from my spot for fear he will take it as a sign of encouragement.

I start to breathe again as he and his Harley pull out. Before I can turn toward our door, Andrew takes my arm. I realize that he had parked his bike on the other side of the lot. He has undoubtedly been watching my interaction with Mark. *Now what?*

"Maggie, please, I really want to talk to you. What did I do wrong? I am not asking to come in because I don't want to upset your husband but please, Maggie, talk to me."

"My husband? You think I'd sleep with you if I were married? Go away, Andrew. Do not call me again ever."

I slam the door to our room. Larry looks at me with concern. I've got a lot of explaining to do. Today has not gone as I had expected. Explaining things to my girlfriends will not go any easier.

Chapter Twenty-Seven

I intend to focus on my job, friends, garden, and bike. Early summer is a beautiful time to be in the Pacific Northwest. It can get very warm in late summer, which is why I wanted the vented jacket, but June can be perfect for riding. Andrew had sent flowers, but I didn't acknowledge them. On our walk Monday evening I give the Cliff Notes version of the Wenatchee to Oroville ride. I state in no uncertain terms that Andrew will be out of my life. I'm not sure my friends understand my reaction. Claire wants to know more about Mark. She thinks I should give him a chance. Megan thinks I should sleep with both of them to make up for lost time. It is her opinion that women should treat men like sex objects. That does make me laugh. I've tried to explain I'm just not that kind of woman. Denise keeps warning me about needing protection. Larry agrees with Claire, and Ed says I just need to give myself time to decide what I really want. Andrew thinks he knows everything about me, but he has proven that he doesn't. I don't want to spend time with anyone who has such a low opinion of me. Maybe he has a low opinion of all women, but I don't care. Let him find a woman who will put up with that garbage. Mark seemed like a nice man, intelligent and funny. He just tried a little too hard to get into my pants. I can't do that. *You did sleep with Andrew on your first and only real date. I don't want to think about that. I just want to forget it ever happened. But it did, and you know it.*

The phone is ringing on Tuesday evening as I come in the door after work. I try not to sound breathless as I answer.

"Hi, Maggie, did I catch you at a bad time?" It is Mark. I can't say that I am totally surprised that he is calling. I assume he got my number from Larry.

"Mark, what a surprise. I just walked in the door. It has been a very busy day. Could you call me back in about fifteen minutes? My cat thinks he needs to be fed and will be a pest if I don't do that." Fifteen minutes will also give me enough time to catch my breath, and finally decide what I want to do about Mark.

"Fifteen minutes, it will be," I stand for a few seconds with the phone in my hand taking deep breaths in an effort to clear my mind. Murphy Jones, the cat, reminds me that I had not lied to Mark. I lay down the phone and walk with Murphy to fill his food bowl. A multitude of thoughts race through my mind. *Maybe Larry and Claire are correct. We didn't really get a chance to talk at the concert. Talking to Mark is not like I'm planning to sleep with the man. Okay, I hadn't planned to sleep with Andrew, but I did. Sleeping with him does not mean we are going steady, so dating Mark is not like I'm two-timing Andrew. Do people even talk about going steady anymore? Oh, I really don't know how to date at this age. You know he is going to ask to see you. Make up your mind. Yes, or No?" You know you are only going to say yes to get back at Andrew. He will never know, and I am a grown woman who can get to know any man I want to. Who knows, maybe Mark will become a good friend. Is he really looking for a friend? Maybe both of us can ride our bikes together. Going for rides could be fun. Baby steps; just take baby steps.*

The phone ends my internal discussion. It's showtime. "Hello." Murphy and I settle into a comfy chair.

"Is this better, Maggie?"

"It is. Sorry if I was rude before. My cat is very spoiled and can be so demanding."

Mark laughs. "I've had ex-wives like that. A demanding cat sounds like a much better idea. Tell me about him."

I know he is trying hard to put me at ease. Do I tell him about Murphy, or do I ask him to get to the point? Chatting about Murphy now means the cat won't be a safe topic if I do accept a date. *Don't overthink this, Maggie. He is being friendly. Tell him about your cat.* "He is a four-year-old tabby with an interesting pattern of gray, black, white and tan spots and stripes. He was dumped at my house as a very tiny kitten. I just had to adopt him. Actually, I think he adopted me. Now he thinks he rules the house. Do you have pets?"

"I have a golden lab named Max, who is almost twelve. His muzzle is getting white, but he still is eager to retrieve balls. He loves it when we go down to the river, so he can retrieve them from the water. I think he is disappointed that I am not a duck hunter. If you are a dog person as well as a cat person, I'll have to introduce you to him someday soon."

This is probably where I should say something cute about having a blonde in his life, but for all I know, he has other blondes with only two legs as well. Keep it simple. "Max sounds like a very nice dog. I'd had dogs in the past, but now I settle for dog sitting for a friend who travels a lot for work. Mark, I'm sure you didn't call to talk about our pets."

Mark seems to laugh easily, and I need more of that in my life. "That's not totally true, Maggie, for this second call this evening. I knew you have a cat, so I was curious. I really want to get to know you. Beautiful women don't enter my life as often as you may think. My sense is that you are very much more than just a beautiful woman. I may not have been able to talk you into dinner at my house last time, but I'm hoping you'll agree to dinner this Friday. I'll be in Seattle for a number of meetings. What do you say, Maggie?"

"I'm free on Friday evening. Where would you like to meet for dinner?"

"Well I had thought I could pick you up, and then we could select one of the restaurants around Lake Union."

Don't panic, Maggie. Just be honest about meeting him there. "Mark, you seem like a very nice man, but I'd be more comfortable if I drove myself there. I'm still new to dating at this age. The world has changed since I was a young single woman. I need to take things very slowly."

"I understand. You must have thought I was too pushy last time. I'm happy that you are giving me a second chance. What kind of food do you like? Lake Union has lots of seafood options but also some great ethnic choices."

We spend the next ten minutes discussing our tastes in food before agreeing to meet at Duke's Seafood and Chowder on Friday evening at seven. I just made a dinner date with someone who is not Andrew. I wonder what my friends will say. Only much later do I think back to the start of our conversation. *Did he say he had ex-wives? That means more than one. This may not be such a good idea, after all. This is at least better than a blind date from the dating website.*

Chapter Twenty-Eight

Wednesday morning, I awake with the realization that I really don't have anything to wear for a date with Mark. Ed had pulled skirts and blouses from my closet for my date with Andrew, but I think I need a dress. I'll call Ed for help in selecting just the right one at his shop later this afternoon. My second thought was about what, if anything, I would tell my girlfriends about my upcoming date. I really don't want them pushing me into a situation that is more than I can handle. I think I'll leave that discussion for after my date on Friday. By Saturday morning, I'm sure I will be asking for their advice.

I call Ed as I dress for work. I don't want Claire to overhear my plans. I love her, but I want this shopping trip to be all mine. I want something light, fun, but yet conservative. That would not happen with Claire's help. Ed agrees to meet me at his shop around four PM. I should be able to select a dress or two before meeting my friends for our walk night.

Ed greets me at his shop with a big hug. "Oh, Maggie, I'm so happy you decided to shop. I have some new items that I think will be perfect for you. Are you really sure you want just a dress? I'm sure you could use some new skirts and blouses for work as well as dates. I wasn't wrong about that outfit I put together for your date with Andrew, was I?"

"That combination was wonderful, but for this dinner, I really want a dress. With Mark, I don't want it to appear too easy for him to try to undress me. Something tells me that it might be best if you could actually sew me in to the dress."

"Oh my! This sounds like an exciting date. Is Mark the one you met on that motorcycle ride?"

"He is. I'm giving him a second chance."

"Larry said that you had been a little upset after riding with Mark. What did he do?"

"Well Mark was moving a little too fast for me, but I was really upset about Andrew."

"Oh yes, Larry told me about Andrew thinking that you and he were married. So Mark made moves on you, and now you're going on a date?"

"I am. I like this dress. Would it look good on me?"

"I think it will be perfect. Let me get a couple more for you to try on."

Ed is right, the dress fits perfectly, and the soft green colored print makes me feel young, and like springtime. Ed also selects another dress in coral with a full skirt that was a little more casual and playful. The third dress was more structured and in a rich Navy blue. I buy all three.

I manage to get through the week without telling my friends about my upcoming date. It was easier than I expected, because Megan was out of town, and Denise was going to her son's baseball game on Friday night. I had forgotten to check the calendar for Friday night pizza before making the date with Mark. We will all get together on Saturday morning for our normal walk time. By that time, I'll be ready to share all the details because I am confident that they won't be too exciting.

Friday morning, I decide to ride Bernie so Claire won't ask about my plans after work. I don't like to lie to her, so I do better if she doesn't even ask. I reach home with just enough time to shower, put on my dress, dry my hair, and put on some makeup. Once in my car and driving to Seattle, I have more than enough time to panic. *Why did I ever agree to a dinner with Mark? Do I really need another Harley riding man in my life? Andrew has given me enough grief about riding a scooter. Won't Mark be the same way?*

Duke's has been on Lake Union for decades. They have several restaurants on the waterfront in different Seattle locations. The Lake Union restaurant is one of the oldest. Like many other restaurants in the area, they are building a larger upscale version that will still be on the lake but with more parking. Tonight, I'm lucky to find a parking spot someone else has just vacated in the lot closest to the restaurant. At least, I don't have to struggle with a long walk in heels. Now to find Mark.

Mark is waiting for me at the front door. "Maggie, it is so good to see you. You just sparkle when you smile." He gives me a quick hug and kiss on my cheek. I'm just happy that his hands do not wander in the wrong directions.

"Thank you, Mark. It is good to see you as well." Duke's on a Friday night is always packed. At least happy hour is over, so the noise level has dropped a bit. We are shown to a table with a view of the lake. I assume he made that reservation well in advance. No Lake Union restaurant ever has enough lake view tables.

"I've been eating at Duke's whenever I'm in Seattle for years. The view of the Columbia River in Wenatchee pales in comparison to the view of Lake Union or the Puget Sound. I'm so glad I can share this with you. You live south of the city, don't you?"

"I do. In our area, we have Salty's in Redondo and Anthony's Homeport in Des Moines, which are both on the Sound. There is something about water views that is just so relaxing. Do you get to Seattle often?"

"I'm here for meetings at least once a month. This next week I'll be back twice to observe instructors that we may be interested in hiring. I also enjoy coming for a weekend on my Harley. When we first met, you mentioned that you had your own bike. Tell me about it."

Before I can do that, our server asked to take our drink order. Mark asks, "Would you like wine with dinner? I could order a bottle."

"I think for tonight I'll stick with iced tea, thank you." The last thing I need tonight is a repeat of my behavior after two glasses of wine over that dinner with Andrew. Look how that turned out.

"So you are going to tell me about your bike. Do you ride a Harley?"

Well, here we go, "No, I ride a Bergman 650 scooter. It is hardly a powerful motorcycle like a Harley, but I've just learned to ride. I had decided that I needed the extra help that a scooter gives me."

"Wow, a scooter. A 650 would give you the power for a serious ride. Maybe the next time I'm over, we could do just that. My first choice would be to have you wrap your arms around me on my Harley again, but seeing you on your own bike might be fun as well. What color is your Bergman?"

"I had wanted red, but it is gray. I settled for red on my helmet instead."

"I remember your red helmet. It suits you. Now, what looks good for dinner?"

We agreed to share the crab cake appetizer followed by macadamia encrusted halibut for each of us. An hour later, I am surprised at how easy it had been to chat with Mark as we ate. "So, Maggie," he asks as we walked to my car, "will you have dinner with me when I'm in town next week?"

"I'll need to check my schedule. Some evenings I have late escrow signings, but if that's not the case, I'd love to have dinner with you."

"Let's chat during the week. Maybe I should ride my bike, so we could have an early dinner at Snoqualmie Falls. Hopefully, that isn't too far for you to ride. Of course, you could always ride with me on my Harley."

"I should be able to make that ride. It sounds like fun. Now it's time for me to head home. I had a great time, Mark. Thank you." Before I can get into my car, Mark pulls me into his arms and kisses me. It's a gentle brush of the lips, a sweet kiss. He doesn't try to make it more than that, and his hands stay above my waist. I'll have enough to tell my friends in the morning. I can also tell Ed that he would not have needed to sew me into the dress. Maybe I can do this dating thing, after all.

Chapter Twenty-Nine

Our walk on Saturday morning starts like many others. Megan tells us about the dates she had during her week in Tampa. She still hasn't found a keeper, but she intends to keep trying. Denise talks about her son Tyler, and his desire to start shaving at age eleven. She is concerned that he is trying to grow up too fast. Claire shares that her husband Mike is talking about quitting his job. She's afraid he might have a new girlfriend. Fearing I'll just blurt out about my date with Mark, I keep quiet, listening to their stories, without commenting. Denise is the first to notice. "Maggie, you haven't said a word this morning. That is so unlike you. What's going on?"

Claire stops and turns to look at me. "Maggie, did you have another fight with Andrew?"

"I know," Megan exclaims, "you and Andrew had sex again. You know we will make you talk about it. Claire may be willing to settle for the highlights, but I want the details."

Shaking my head, I keep my pace even and continue listening as we resume walking. "I'll bet that this has nothing to do with Andrew," Denise says. "If it was about him, she would have told us by now. This is something different."

Claire says, "If you are considering doing something silly, you need to share with us. We are your friends, and we want to help."

I realize that my friends know me too well. "You remember that I told you about Doctor Mark Johnson after the Wenatchee motorcycle ride with Larry. He called this week, and I had dinner with him last night. I've agreed to see him again this next week."

Megan is the first to ask, "So did you have two glasses of wine, and have sex with him?"

"No, I did not have sex with him. I have learned my lesson and stayed with iced tea during dinner. I love all of you, but I wanted to make certain that my decision to have dinner with him was actually my idea. Sometimes the three of you can be a bit pushy. Remember my coffee date with the real estate developer? I don't think I would have ever agreed to that, if you hadn't pushed. Dinner with Mark was my decision. I even bought a new dress with only Ed's help. And just for the record, I don't intend to talk to Andrew in the near future if ever. Next week Mark will be back on this side of the mountains, and we will go for a motorcycle ride together. He's talking about Snoqualmie Falls for dinner."

Claire says, "What if he books a room at the Inn there? Maybe he plans to have you for dinner."

"Come on now, I'm not twenty. I do know how to say no."

Denise mumbles under her breath, "You didn't say no to Andrew."

"I heard that. Andrew was two glasses of wine. I won't make that mistake with Mark."

"I'll bet Mark isn't as sexy as Andrew. Just the thought of that man, makes me drool. Oh well, Mark will be good practice for you," Claire says. "Will you be riding behind on Mark's Harley?"

"No, I'll be on my own bike."

Megan chimes in, "That won't be as much fun as pressing your breasts into the man's back as you wrap your arms around him."

"Enough about Andrew, Mark, and my sex life. Let's talk about something else."

"Killjoy." We continue our walk.

It doesn't rain at all during the next week. I am able to ride my scooter to work each day. Federal Way to

Snoqualmie Falls will be a long ride for me as well as dealing with Friday night traffic. I'm feeling more confident with the additional riding. Mark will come south from the University of Washington to meet at my office at 4 PM on Friday. The northbound rush hour traffic would still be difficult with my level of riding experience. From my office, we will travel Highway 18 east toward Maple Valley, on the same route I had taken with Mike Smith. We will continue on Highway 18 over Tiger Mountain pass. There will still be lots of traffic but not as heavy as on the Interstate. It also has a lot of sharp curves. It should be a scenic ride. On my return trip, I may take the Interstate as a faster route. Most of the rush hour should be over by then. I didn't ask Mark where he was staying. It might open a door that I don't want to go through. I don't want him to think I'm considering spending the night with him. This date is for dinner only. I just hope he knows that.

I hear the roar of Mark's Harley before he even pulls into the parking lot. Claire must have heard it too because she comes into our office and is standing by Annie's desk. My first thought is to meet Mark outside, but I know Annie and Claire would just follow me. As Mark comes through the door, I am struck by how good he looks in his leathers. I try not to compare him to Andrew, but that is difficult. Both men are tall and slim with a full head of hair. Mark's hair has much more silver, and his eyes are a deep brown rather than Andrew's blue. "Mark, it's good to see you. How was traffic on your ride down from the University?"

"I'll admit that traffic in Wenatchee is significantly less than Seattle. Seattle, however, still pales when compared with Los Angeles. So introduce me to these two beautiful ladies," Mark says with a smile. The man is clearly a flirt.

Annie giggles as I make the introductions. Claire just smiles, but she raises her eyebrows when she turns toward me. I'm really glad that I can't hear her thoughts out loud. "Let me get my keys and bag, and then I will be ready to go. Annie, I will see you on Monday. Claire, I'll see you in the morning for our walk."

As I walked to the door, Claire says, "Just give me a call if you can't make it in the morning." I hear Claire and Annie giggling as I continue out the door.

Mark walks around my bike before saying, "That's a nice-looking ride. It's not a Harley, but I bet it's fun to ride. One of these days, you will have to let me try it out. Why don't we plan to stop at the top of Tiger Mountain. You might want a short break before we go all the way to the Snoqualmie."

"You're right. I might need to stretch my legs there."

Traffic is manageable from Federal Way through Auburn on Highway 18. Once past Maple Valley, the road opens to rolling hills and fir trees. As we wind our way up Tiger Mountain, I think about the logging trucks that had been a main fixture on the highway in years gone past. I'm sad for all the loggers who lost their jobs, but I don't miss sharing the road with all of those big trucks. The pullout on the right side at the top of the mountain is not as large as the big parking lot on the left. Both pullouts, however, are gravel with lots of potholes. I carefully select a place to park. Mark parks beside me. We pull off our helmets so we can talk. "Your scooter really held its own on the way up. I like the way you leaned into the curves. Tiger Mountain isn't as high as Snoqualmie Pass, but I bet you could drive it without an issue. You will soon be ready to make the ride to Wenatchee."

It almost sounds like he has respect for me and my bike. "Thank you. I will confess that I needed to stop here just to unclench my hands. The Bergman handles the curves and hills, but I still get tense."

"It is good to learn to relax while you ride, but never get too comfortable. You need to be alert to ride safely. Are you ready to continue?"

"I am," I say as I pull on my red helmet.

Chapter Thirty

Snoqualmie is a popular name in this area of Washington. There is the 3,100 foot Snoqualmie Pass which divides Washington into its western and eastern parts via Interstate 90. Thirty-five miles west of the pass is the city of Snoqualmie with its winery, golf course, and railroad. Adjacent to the city is Snoqualmie Falls. Although not the tallest waterfall in Washington, it is one of the most picturesque. Because it is so close to Seattle, it has over a million visitors each year. There has been a lodge overlooking the falls since 1916. It has been remodeled and expanded a number of times over the years. It is now called the Salish Inn and Spa. It had been updated with modern rooms, a spa, and two restaurants, and yet it still maintains a warm cozy lodge feeling. Originally, the Inn was known for its hearty breakfast, but now it offers full service in both casual and formal dining. The Inn even offers the Chefs Studio with cooking classes and private dining. Mark and I both agree that the more casual restaurant would work best. I couldn't see myself in the formal dining room wearing leather pants. The least I can do is remove my helmet, do-rag, and riding jacket before we enter.

As soon as we are settled, Mark asks, "Are you ready to have a glass of wine with our dinner?"

"Wine would normally depend on what we were ordering for dinner. Tonight, however, I'm riding, so no wine for me."

"Well, if you don't feel comfortable driving home after a glass of wine, I could book us a room here, and you could go home in the morning."

I can't suppress my laugh. "Nice try, but I'll pass on both."

Mark laughs as well, "It was worth a try. What do you think about an order of clams, followed by a pizza?"

"That sounds wonderful. The wild mushroom pesto pizza sounds intriguing."

"It does, so let's do that."

It is easy to chat with Mark as we wait for our appetizer. He shares many entertaining stories about being a bull rider, traveling the world for Exxon Mobil, and his switch to education. I laugh a lot as I share stories about hiking in the Cascade Mountains and how the volume of water over the falls changes during the year. More than anything else, I try not to remember the weekends Jim and I had spent here. The last thing I need to do is cry over my late husband during this dinner with Mark.

Mark reaches across the table to take my hand, "Maggie, you have suddenly gotten very quiet. What are you thinking about?"

Taking a deep breath, I start, "My late husband and I stayed here at the Inn when our children were small. They are good memories." At least I can say that without tears.

"I hadn't thought about you having a husband. Larry said you were single, and I had assumed you were divorced. How long ago did you lose your husband?"

"It has been a year and a half, and to be honest I still miss him. I'll probably always miss him; we were married for over thirty years. They were very good years, and we have two beautiful children. If you don't mind, let's change the subject. Do you have children?"

Our pizza has arrived. Mark gently changes the subject as he says, "The clams were amazing, but this pizza almost looks like a work of art. My son is a chef at an upscale restaurant in Houston. I think he became a foodie after sampling different cuisines in the countries we traveled to when he was younger. I don't see him as often as I would like, but he seems to be happy with his life. I can't ask for more."

"Well, the pizza tastes as good as it looks. My son and daughter are not foodies, but I do hope they could appreciate this type of pizza. My son is just out of college, and my daughter has small children. I'm sure they have seen their share of pepperoni in recent years."

Mark laughs. "You are much too young to be a grandmother. Tell me about them."

We continue to talk and laugh about our children, our jobs, and riding our bikes. I feel Jim's presence as a warm glow. As we finish our pizza, I realize two things. Mark is a very nice man, who I'm sure will become a good friend. More importantly, I don't feel the sparks that I had when talking with Andrew. I have to let Mark know that this will be our last date. I start by telling him that it is time for me to hit the road. I've decided to take I-90 to I-5 through Seattle. Mark says he will be riding on to Wenatchee. He gives me a gentle kiss before I pull on my red helmet. We wave as we head in opposite directions at the Freeway. Dating and riding the freeways; I can do this.

Chapter Thirty-One

Destination Harley is sponsoring a Ride for the Fallen poker run from Tacoma to Pacific Beach out on the Washington coast. It sounds like fun and is for a good cause once again. I never realized how much money the motorcycle clubs and stores raised for charity. Harley riders are known for their rough biker gangs. Motorcycle riders and especially Harley riders have a reputation for hard drinking and girls who pull their T-shirts up, but there is a whole different side as well. New Harleys, like Goldwings, can be very expensive for a hobby. They are not bikes for unemployed teenagers. How many lawyers like Andrew ride bikes? Of course, Andrew did look really grungy when I first saw him. I never did ask him why he had that three-day growth. We never talked after I found out who he was. Maybe I don't really know him any more than he knows me. Have I made a mistake about how I have treated him? That is something to consider.

The best things about a poker run are that there is no time limit, and there are seven required stops to pick up playing cards along the way. I can break the hundred-mile trip into as many long stops as I need. Sue had called to tell me that a number of the women from our ride to Silverdale have decided to join this run. We don't plan to ride as a group, but we can start that way. She suggested that she and I ride our bikes together.

I arrive well before the 10 AM registration time. Sue joins me a little bit later, as do the other women from our prior ride. We want to be in the first departure group. There are other women as well who are riding on a bike with a man. We chat as we stand in line for the ladies' room. Some of the women are complaining that their man does not like to stop along the way for any reason other than to pick up their cards. Sue gives a hearty laugh. "That is why I ride for myself. I love the feeling of independence and confidence I get from firing up my own bike. I also love that I can stop whenever I want without having to beg."

"I never said I had to beg," one of the women says.

"No, but you are not in control either. Of course, it is a little harder for a woman to head to the bushes along the road than it is for a man!"

"They also don't need to stand in a line for a restroom."

"They just don't get the chance to make friends like we do."

We are all laughing and giggling as we chat.

Back at our bikes, we grab our helmets as we watch a group of Goldwing riders head out. Sue and I fall in behind them. The other women are in pairs behind us. More bikes are pulling up to the registration table as we leave. Bikers will continue to start in groups every fifteen minutes until noon. The ride will take between two and three hours. The rule of the road for these rides is five miles an hour below the speed limit for safety. The first leg of the trip will be down Interstate 5 to Olympia, where we will exit to head west. Sue is right; I do feel independent and confident as I merge with traffic on the Interstate. I guess I'm not too old to enjoy the ride.

We make the stop at Olympia for our cards. I take a short walk around before getting back on my bike. Sue does the same. I had been tense as we rode past the Fort Lewis complex just south of Tacoma. The traffic was slow there, where a car-truck accident had occurred. Vehicles don't seem to see the bike and cut very close. I try to remember to breathe, but it isn't easy. The break helps. Highway 8 will also help because it is more rural with tall trees lining the divided highway. I am learning that I love scenic drives.

At the third stop, Sue says she needs a ladies' room break. As we walk back to our bikes, she shares something with me. "I didn't really need the ladies' room, but it is the only place I could think of that gives us a reprieve from the roar of motorcycles. I love my Harley but I wish I had gone with a Goldwing simply because they are just a little bit quieter. That was the real reason I wanted to be in the first wave. I knew from past rides that the Goldwing group is always first in line. From here on out, the waves will become more intermixed, and the decibels will go up. I've been doing poker runs for years. They are fun, but I'm too old to enjoy the noise." By now, I am laughing so hard I almost tip my bike. I have been thinking the same thing. Mark's Harley had been one of the extra loud ones. On the Run for the Border ride, the bikes were spread out over a long stretch of highway. Here we were starting and stopping often, which means the bikes are revved up before pulling out. The sound level also revved up. At least my scooter doesn't add much to that roar.

As we mount up, I see a familiar Harley Road King. Andrew gives me a little wave as he comes to a stop. I don't want to look again as I pull out, but I do need to check that direction for other riders. *God, he does look good in leathers. Maybe I should just sleep with him for the good sex. Oh, what are you thinking?*

We arrive in Pacific Beach after riding for two hours and forty-five minutes. I'm tired, but not exhausted. Most of the stops were very quick ones where we didn't even park as we picked up our cards. Maybe I will do a poker run again, but Sue really is right about the noise. The parking lot is filling quickly with motorcycles. I park my scooter beside Sue's trike. After turning in our cards, we walk into the hotel. The group has reserved a conference room with a bar as well as tables and chairs as people wait for the last group of riders to complete the run. There will be prizes for the top winning hands. Sue finds a place to settle, and I continue over to the hotel registration. I had made the reservation as soon as I decided on doing this ride. I knew I would not be ready to ride back on the same day. I had packed a change of clothes, and more importantly, a pair of sandals for a couple of walks on the beach. I wish my friends could have met me here, but we all have busy lives. Maybe next time.

My room is comfortable and cozy. The hotel originally opened as a retreat for military families and later expanded to include the general public. They still give a discount for active military personnel, which is nice with so many bases near Seattle. I am just happy that I could book a room. After changing, I join Sue at the conference center. My riding gear is comfortable, but wearing a T-shirt and jeans is more relaxing, and my sandals are better for the beach. Sue has a big glass of iced tea, because she says she just can't drink a beer and then drive. We laugh about having the tea and how many stops she will need to make before she is back home. "Since I don't have to either drive or make stops, I'm getting a glass of wine. Are you sure you don't want to stay the night? We could share my room. They did give me one with two queen beds."

"I'll be fine after I rest just a bit and have a burger with some of the boys. They can be a fun group. Some of us have even made the ride to Sturgis, South Dakota, together. That place is incredible. Instead of having the streets lined with gold, they are lined with miles and miles of bikes in all of the towns in the Black Hills. Have you been there?"

"My late husband and I took the kids when they were younger. We did all of the tourist stops in the Black Hills, but we didn't do it in the first week of August. I have heard that cars can't even drive through some of the towns. Do they really close the streets so only bikes can park?

How do they handle that many people? Do the women actually lift their shirts as often as I've heard?"

"Only the young women do that, Dearie, only the young ones. You see all sorts of bikes, biker chicks, and crusty old men. It is no longer just a hard-drinking Harley event, although there are probably more Harleys than any other brand. No one would say a thing about you and your scooter. It is all about the love of riding, and of course the music at all of the concerts. I'm not going this year, but you might want to think about going. I'm not sure I really want to make that long ride again. There are a number of people who will trailer their bikes and then just ride into town to show them off. That is the way I'd probably go the next time. You could do the same thing."

I find it hard to breathe when Andrew strides into the conference room. He stops at a table of mostly women to chat for a few minutes. The women's laughter can be heard over the other noises in the room. One is blushing while one covers her mouth as she leans toward another woman. He is obviously successful as a flirt. *Screw him.*

After the prizes are awarded for the winning hands, I say good-bye to Sue and walk down to the beach. I really want to dig my toes into the sand, listen to the sea birds, and think about anything other than Andrew. I'm not sure Sue is correct about how my scooter would be accepted at Sturgis, but if I were to go, it would be the only sensible way to get around. I just can't see myself joining that many Harleys. Am I even thinking about making such a trip for Andrew or for myself? What do I really want for my life?

Chapter Thirty-Two

I am watching the waves as I hear Andrew's voice behind me, "Hi, Maggie. I didn't know that you would be making this ride. I know you have been avoiding me. Can we talk?"

My first impulse is to yell at him to go away. Instead, I take a deep breath. I can't run away forever. I need to hear him out. "I'm not sure what you can say that I want to hear, but go ahead."

"I'm really sorry for upsetting you. I don't know why you ran out of my house or why you wouldn't accept my calls. I honestly assumed that you must have been married to Larry. I also thought you would find it funny that I knew you rode a scooter. I don't understand what's going on here."

"Larry is my friend and neighbor. If he were to get married, I know it would be to his partner Ed. They have been together for a long time. I didn't run out of your house. I told you that my children come over on Saturday mornings. To be honest, though, you are the first man I've been with since my husband, Jim, died. It was just too much for me. You might have been right when you said that you thought I was married, because at that moment I still felt like I was married. I was cheating on my husband even though he was dead. This probably doesn't make any sense to you."

Reaching out, Andrew brushes the hair from my eyes. "And I was rushing you. You are a beautiful woman, Maggie, and I can't help being attracted to you. Kissing you just seems right, and there didn't seem to be any reason to stop. We aren't kids, Maggie. When I screw up, you need to tell me, not shut me out. I may not have had much respect for a scooter, but you learned how to ride with your special style shining through, and I'm proud of you. Can you forgive me? Can we start over?"

God, the man has a voice that makes me want to pull off his clothes, and a look in those blue eyes that goes right through me. So, what do I do now? Time for a deep breath, "Hi, I'm Maggie King. Have we met?"

Andrew starts laughing as he pulls me close for a kiss. A wave crashes in at that moment, soaking us to our knees. His riding boots have filled with water. He still manages to laugh as he kisses me again. I can't keep my toes from curling. "Let's head up to my room where we can dry off before we drown."

He rubs his thumb across my lips. "That only works if I can keep kissing you. I love the way you taste."

"I really don't want you to stop."

When we reach the dry sand, he pulls off his boots. Before I can offer to help, he loses his balance and lands on his back in the sand, pulling me down on top of him. We are both laughing like children until he slides his hands up my body to take my face. He looks so serious as he kisses me. Flipping me, so he is on top, he holds my hands out to the side as he gently bites my nipple through my T-shirt. Instantly, I am wet, and need so much more. There is no time for thought. "My room. Now!"

He grabs his boots and follows as I run for the steps up to the hotel. I stop to catch my breath before leading the way down the hall.

I fumble the key at the door. "Let me do that" as he takes the key from my hand.

We no more than close the door before I pull his T-shirt over his head and reach for his belt buckle. Pulling my T-shirt off and unhooking my bra, his teeth return to their action from the beach. Quickly stepping out of my jeans, my body starts to melt as he eases me back on to the bed and then joins me. "Now, please, now. I want you inside me."

He does just that quickly matching his thrusts to mine, faster and faster until I orgasm in an explosion of stars. He follows right behind me and drops down beside me. *That was just what I wanted and needed. Why did I run away from this before?*

"I find myself thinking about Rip VanWinkle right now," Andrew says between deep breaths.

"Rip VanWinkle? I can't think at all, and you are thinking about Rip VanWinkle? I have to know, why old Rip?"

"As I remember the story, Rip's wife died after a fit of passion. I never thought that was a fit of anger but actual passion. If we had met thirty years ago, we would probably have followed in her footsteps. I had planned to take things slow, because I didn't want to scare you away again. If this was slow, I'm in serious trouble. I'm not twenty anymore, hell, I'm not even fifty. Maybe in two, three, or better yet four hours, we can try this again, but let's slow it down. Raw sex is great, but next time, I want to make love to you. I want to get to know every inch of you." He is running his fingers through my hair.

I roll onto my side to face him. I trace a path on his chest with my fingertip. My breathing has not yet slowed to normal. My voice still comes out a little raspy. "I can do slow. We have discovered we are still capable of your 'fit of passion' but slow sounds wonderful. Do you think we can take a shower, and then go for another walk on the beach before having dinner at the restaurant? I think I have sand in places that were never meant to have sand."

"The shower, a walk, then food sound perfect. Although, if we did the walk before the shower, I'd have time to think of ways to remove that sand for you. Who knows, I might just recover by then!"

"Tempting as that may be, I think I want a shower alone before I put on my wet jeans. While I'm doing that, you might want to see how wet your boots are. Taking a shower with you might get something started that I don't have the energy to finish at this time."

"Do you always try to be practical?"

"Only if it means I get the shower first!"

Andrew had shaken the sand from our jeans while I shower. They were damp but manageable. He had placed the rest of our clothes in a chair. I brush more sand from my underwear as I call the restaurant to make a dinner reservation. As Andrew is getting out of the shower, I call the front desk to request a few more towels.

"You didn't have to rush getting dressed. I haven't had nearly enough time to just look at you. I like the look of you dressed, but undressed is even better."

"I can understand a man wanting to look at the body of a twenty-something, but a fifty-five-year-old woman after having had two children is not the same. "

"Twenty-somethings can be beautiful, but you have lived life. That is much more interesting, and you are just plain gorgeous."

I'll admit that I enjoy the view as he dresses. He must go to a gym or do something besides sit at a desk for him to keep the muscles in his shoulders so defined. He could have posed for Michelangelo. All parts of him look just as good.

I snap out of my reverie when, he asks if I have my key. It is tucked safely in my pocket. The tide is going out so we have a much wider path of wet sand to walk well away from the waves. A feeling of peace and contentment wraps around me as the sea birds take flight ahead of us as we stroll hand in hand.

About a half-mile down the beach, Andrew pulls me into his arms and gives me a playful smile. "How much time do we have before our dinner reservations?" He raises his eyebrows as he widens his smile. Before I can answer, he has started to kiss my neck. He slides his hands up from my waist to cup my breasts. My breath catches as my nipples harden. This man is like a drug.

"If we turn around right now, we will have just enough time to finish this," I answer with a giggle.

"Really?" He sounds a little skeptical.

"Oh, yes. If we head back to the room now, I know just where you left your boots, and I left my sandals. Once we have those on, it will be time for dinner."

Andrew throws his head back laughing. "I did say I wanted to take things slow, and that I need two or three hours to recover. Let's go have dinner." Giving me a quick kiss, he takes my hand as we walk back to the hotel.

Over dinner, we exchange stories about work and friends. I ask about that three-day growth he was sporting when I first saw him. "I had finished a big case and had gone for a long bike ride with friends. We rode to Montana to a fishing cabin. I didn't need to shave until I went back to work the following week. My friends like to tease me about my clean-cut lawyer life. When I don't have to be in court, I like to let my beard grow. Someday I may actually try a full beard and mustache." I realize there are lots of things that I don't know about the man.

Finally, as we start on a shared dessert, Andrew addresses the elephant in the room. "Tell me about your husband."

"Where do I start? His name was Jim, and we were married for thirty years. He was a wonderful husband and father. He died almost two years ago of lung cancer. It took us both by surprise. He thought he just had a cold or allergies that left him with a cough. He was gone in just eight weeks after the diagnosis. It has been hard for me to adjust to life without him. We had had big plans for our future."

I try to keep my voice level as I continue. "He had dirt bikes when we were first married. I was happy when he got rid of them. A few years ago, he bought an older Harley that he spent hours fixing. He was able to ride it a few times before someone made him an offer to buy it. He didn't feel he could afford to refuse the offer. He had said he hoped we could ride together once he had the bike running, but didn't think the Harley was the right bike for that. I was surprised when he decided to buy a new Goldwing. We took the safety class together so I could be a better passenger while he got his endorsement. We started making plans for a cross-country trip just before we learned he had cancer. The bike sat in the garage for a year before I was ready to sell it. The sale had just been completed when I first saw you at Hindshaw's."

Andrew has taken my hand while I talk. I am proud of myself that I didn't break down in tears. The pain was there so sharp I didn't think I could face it. "I'm so sorry for your loss, Maggie. That must have been very hard to do. So why did you decide to buy a scooter?"

"I selected a scooter because it was more manageable for an older woman just learning to ride. I had really loved the feeling I got when we had ridden the Goldwing. I can't put that into words. It goes beyond a sense of freedom. It was also a way to remember the good times. After I started riding, I have become hooked on the independence. I feel whole again."

"Let's go for another walk before we go back to your room. This time I really am going to make slow, gentle love to you."

Chapter Thirty-Three

My body always knows when it is 6 AM, even when I wish it didn't. I'm awake. At home, 6 AM is helped by the smell of fresh coffee that I preprogrammed the night before. The smell of the ocean reminds me that I'm not at home. Having Andrew's arm around me is a second reminder. This feels good. I am able to push my mother's voice out of my head before she even gets started. I'm a grown single woman who can have wild sex and share my bed with a man if I want. The sex wasn't actually wild, but it was fabulous and fun. The ladies will approve. My toes curl just thinking about it.

I'd really like to snuggle in, but the thought of coffee just won't go away. There is a coffee maker in the corner of the room. It keeps calling my name. Maybe I can slide out without waking Andrew. "Where are you going? You aren't trying to run away, are you? This is your room, not mine."

"I'm going to make coffee. Would you like a cup?"

"Only if I don't need to open my eyes. What time is it anyway?"

"Early. Go back to sleep. You can have coffee when you are actually awake."

After starting the coffee, I step outside to watch the ocean. The beach is filled with shorebirds, who dance away as a wave crashes in. It is a sight I always enjoy. Further out there is a freighter heading north possibly toward Seattle via the Strait of Juan de Fuca or maybe on to Alaska. The morning fog still clings to shore in places, but it looks like it will be a nice day. I shouldn't have to worry about wind or rain on my ride home.

I jump when Andrew kisses the back of my neck. "Your coffee, my lady."

"I didn't realize that you were up. I tried to be quiet so you could go back to sleep."

"The bed felt empty without you, and this is when I usually get up. See, we have something else in common. You, however, seem to actually be awake. I am up, but it takes me a while to truly wake up."

"This has always been my favorite time of the day. When the children were small, it was the only time I had to myself. Here the peaceful sound of the waves is too good to miss. Of course, you have that every day at your new house. Have you gotten more settled?"

"I have furniture, but I still haven't gotten unpacked. I have a big case coming up, so it has kept me more than occupied. In fact, I need to head back fairly soon to get notes organized for a meeting in the morning. Let's go have some breakfast, and we can ride back together if you are ready."

"Breakfast sounds good. "

Over eggs and bacon, Andrew tells me about his case. I'd never really thought much about corporate law. I have watched Rizzoli & Isles or Law and Order on and off for years, and they don't always portray the criminal attorney in a very good light. I can't see Andrew as sleazy as those lawyers. "Why corporate law?"

"When I was a kid, my Uncle Max bought the business where he worked. It had been a handshake deal. The seller said he wanted to retire. He hadn't told the truth. He had stopped paying his suppliers. They wouldn't do business with Max until he paid the back bills. The seller opened a new version of the business a month later down the street. He tried to take the entire old customer base with him. Max learned that he really needed an attorney. He sued to try to recover on the back bills. The seller claimed it was part of the sale. Unfortunately, for the seller, he had bragged to those same suppliers that he had cheated my uncle. It took Uncle Max a long time to get the business on solid footing, but he and his attorney had become lifelong friends. Sounds like a soap opera, but that is when I decided I wanted to be a lawyer."

"Wow, you are right. It does sound like a soap opera. Do you get to play the hero often?"

"Not quite like that, but when I first started out, I worked on a case for a small company in Bothell who objected when Microsoft included their software in DOS 6.0 before Microsoft paid for it. Microsoft took the software out in version 6.1 and put it back in for 6.2 after signing the check. On a lighter note, I won't really have much downtime this next week. Would you like to try for a movie next Sunday? I'm sure we can find something we would both like to see."

"A movie should be fun. This will be a chance to discover what each of us likes in movies. I'll confess to a fondness for romantic comedies and a dislike of blood and guts."

"Maybe we can find a good storyline. There are a few of them out there. Are we ready to ride back?"

"I'll get my things packed. I'll meet you at the bikes in five minutes."

The ride back is relaxed and comfortable. We do stop at the rest area outside of Olympia, but I don't need any additional stops before we say good-bye just after my exit. I now know I can make at least a hundred-mile ride. Unfortunately, my daughter Sharon is waiting for me when I get home. "Mother, where have you been? You go off on that damn bike without telling me or answering your phone. What if we had an emergency? You didn't call me on Saturday night or this morning. I should not need to worry about my mother acting like a teenager."

"I called you Saturday morning. I told you I was going on a ride to the coast, and that I would stay overnight before I came home. Cell reception is spotty out there, and I can't use the phone while I'm riding, so I did turn it off. I knew where to find you if I changed my plans. So, did you have an emergency?"

"No. That isn't the point. This midlife crisis of yours just doesn't make any sense. Won't you please sell this bike?"

"Sorry, Honey. That isn't going to happen. What if I plan a BBQ for family and both new and old friends? There are people I'd really like you to meet. Maybe then you will know I'm not alone in my love of this bike."

"Will you make both kinds of potato salad?"

"I have two children, don't I? Two kinds of potato salad, chicken, and burgers with the works. You could make Grandma's recipe for baked beans. I'm thinking two weeks from now. You can help me plan everything we will need."

"So, who are the new friends?"

"Let's wait and have that be a surprise."

I love to entertain. Making tons of food to share with friends and family is a delight. When Jim was alive, I planned a get together at least once every three months. I was the queen of finding odd holidays to celebrate. Maybe it is time to start doing that once again. There isn't enough time to plan for July 4th, but Bastille Day would work. July 14th is in the middle of the week, but the following weekend would give me enough time to research French foods to add to the menu. I usually like to serve Washington wines, but maybe I should switch to French to carry the French theme. I'll put Sharon on menu research. I'll create the guest list and send the invitations. New and old friends together should make for a good mix.

Chapter Thirty-Four

I can always count on my girlfriends to arrive early on party night. They are quick to spot those little jobs that need to be completed while I take a shower and change my clothes. The tables are set, the food laid out, and we have time for a relaxing glass of wine before Sharon arrives with Thomas and the children. I manage to get a quick kiss from the little ones before they're out the back door, heading for the swing set. Sharon hands Thomas a glass of wine before he follows them. She brings hers into the kitchen to join us.

"What can I do to help?"

"I think we have everything ready, Sharon," Denise says. "Your girls are growing so quickly. I remember when my son was in that cute preschool stage. Now he is preteen and hates everything."

"No, he doesn't, Denise. He is talking to Thomas as they both watch the girls, so he can't hate everything. "

Ed and Larry arrive bringing more food. Sharon adds it to the outside table and starts to fuss about placement and serving spoons. The members of the walking club move toward the far side of the garden as Ed begins to fill them in on the new fashions for fall. They are happy to let Sharon fuss. I join Larry as he greets more neighbors at the front door. They know their way into the house. Larry follows them. Sue pulls in on her trike as Andrew is parking his bike in the driveway. Andrew wraps me in a big hug and deep kiss at the door as my son Richard steps out of his car.

It is time to start the introductions as I turn to hug my son. He whispers in my ear, "So who are the Harley riders?"

"Andrew, I'd like you to meet my son, Richard. Richard, Andrew was an escrow client who also rides, and this is my riding buddy, Sue." I have decided to leave out the fact that I'm actually dating Andrew.

Richard gives me a little smile before turning to Sue and Andrew. "Nice to meet both of you. Great bike, Andrew. Sue, tell me about riding a trike." Richard leads them back out the door to where they have parked their bikes.

I turn to find Sharon right behind me. "Mother, who are those people, and why are they here? Did that biker actually kiss you that way? I don't think I like him. Does he belong to a biker gang? Is that woman a lesbian?"

"I've never asked Sue about her sexual orientation, and I don't care. You sound prejudiced, and I didn't raise you that way. Have more respect for my friends. Andrew is not in a biker gang. He is an attorney who happens to ride a Harley. Now come out where you can actually meet them."

Sharon sighs and gives me a slight eye roll just as she did as a teenager before joining the group out by the bikes. Andrew puts his arm around my shoulders and pulls me in tightly beside him. Before I can say a word, Richard steps in to make the introductions. He knows his sister well, and I love him for it. Sharon remembers to behave herself as she greets both Sue and Andrew. She gives me a sharp look before returning to the house. I'm sure she will burn Thomas's ear in no time. We join my friends and neighbors in the backyard. I can hear Claire laughing, so it is officially a party.

By 10:00 PM most of the food and drink has been consumed, Sharon and Thomas have taken the grandchildren home to bed, and a number of neighbors head out shortly after that. This has been a good party, but now it's my favorite part. I grab a chair closer to the fire pit and put my feet up. During the evening, I've had time to chat with all of my friends and neighbors I don't see very often, but now it is time to enjoy those with whom I'm closest. Megan declares, "It is toast time. Richard, bring the motorcycle discussion group over here to join us." More chairs are arranged around the fire pit. "Maggie, I almost feel like we should start singing campfire songs like we did when we were Girl Scouts. This has been a great evening."

Claire chimes in. "You do know how to organize a get-together, Maggie. You have not lost your touch."

"My turn," Denise says with a lilt in her voice. "Maggie, you've done a great job for this party, but I'm going to award the hero award to Andrew. You seem like a very nice man, but more importantly, I think you actually got Sharon to smile at you. You left the motorcycle discussion just long enough to win her over. Whatever did you talk about with her?"

"Books. We talked about the books that she was reading to the girls. I told her that my mother is an author of children's books. When Sharon said she also liked to make up stories to tell them, I suggested she contact my mother on how to get started writing her own stories."

"Sharon as a writer? I never considered that," Richard says. "When we were kids, she did like to tell me ghost stories, but that was so she could scare me, and then call me a baby."

"Oh, I remember those days. The more you would cry, the more she would tease you. She was very good at that, so she might be a good storyteller. She did major in English. I'd really like to hope that she has something in her life besides her husband and children. It would be wonderful if someone other than me can encourage her. Thank you, Andrew. I hope she does reach out to your mother."

Denise replies, "Changing the topic, Andrew, did I hear you say that you are going to Sturgis? Sue, are you going to go?"

"I'm not going this year, but I have in the past," Sue adds. "The music is great, and it is so much fun to see all of those bikes in one place. I suggested that Maggie go."

Andrew has a smile on his face. "I am going with a group of friends and their wives. It is a long ride but a good one. We don't stay for the whole festival because the trip back is just as long. We take a full two weeks round trip. Would you like to come with us, Maggie?"

I take a deep breath before answering. This is the first time Andrew has met my friends and family. I have not met any of his. Spending two weeks together, 24/7 is a big step. "Wow. I've thought about going to Sturgis, but I don't think I'm ready for that kind of trip on my Bergman."

"On your Bergman?" Andrew laughs. "No, Sturgis is really only for serious bikes like the Harleys Sue, and I have. There may be a few other bikes there, but a scooter would be totally out of place at that kind of rally. Also, that would be entirely too far for a woman like you to ride on your own. I was asking if you wanted to ride on the back of my Harley. You haven't ridden on it yet, but it is a nice cruiser."

"Let me clarify. What do you mean by too far for a woman like me?" I don't even try to keep the ice out of my voice.

Before Andrew can answer, Claire, Megan, and Denise jump to their feet. Megan says, "Great party, Mags, but it is time for us to go. Denise, I think Tyler is still in the family room playing video games. Let's round him up. Maggie, call in the morning if you need help cleaning up. Come, ladies, let's go now."

Richard pulls Sue up. "Sue, say your good-byes. I'll escort you to the door. Mom, I'll call in the morning. Love you." He and Sue make a fast exit.

I'm still staring at Andrew as I give everyone a quick wave. "What did you mean, Andrew?"

"Well, Sue is a more typical woman rider at Sturgis. Her trike is a Harley, and she has ridden for years. She may not be one of the young women who pull up their T-shirts, but she rides with women in her same age group. She can handle herself and her trike," he says with a shake of his head.

He smiles at me, "You ride a scooter for God's sakes. You would be laughed out of town. You are a beautiful professional woman; classy. All I meant is that you should not be there without a man to protect you. If you rode on the back of my bike, we could spend that time together, and you could experience the ultimate bike rally. So do you want to come with me?"

I truly know what it means to see red. "Not only no, but Hell no! I don't need a man to protect me, and I don't need to take a back seat for anyone. If I want to go to Sturgis, I'll take myself on my own bike, thank you very much. Now, Andrew, I think it is time for you to leave. Don't say anything more, just leave now. Don't call me."

"About the time I think you are rational, you prove once again that you are a typical woman. I can see myself out."

At least he doesn't slam the door as he leaves. He makes my blood boil. Time to clean up my kitchen. With no one else here, I can talk to the cat. Murphy Jones doesn't even run away when I raise my voice. A cat rather than a man makes much more sense.

Chapter Thirty-Five

The ladies' walking club has convened early on Sunday morning. They have listened to me rant for the last ten minutes. "This hasn't helped. I still feel angry. I even yelled at the cat last night. Murphy Jones just looked at me and then proceeded to wash himself. Why can't I just get over this and move on? "

Denise asks, "Is that a rhetorical question, or do you want a real answer?"

"Of course, I want a real answer."

"Maybe or maybe not. Promise not to yell at us." Claire says. "Remember, I need to work with you this week. So, with that in mind, the answer is that you are in love with the man. I've been in love and in lust, and it is easy for me to tell the difference, at least on you."

"How can I be in love with a man who makes me so angry by the things he says? He has such a narrow opinion of women, and even narrower of me in particular. I can't be in love with him. It is too soon to be in love with anyone. I should date more men. There must be someone who thinks more like I do than Andrew Simmons."

Megan, Claire, and Denise all answer together, "You are in love with him. He is perfect for you. It is not too soon. Dating others might be fine, but he is the one for you."

Megan takes control of the chatter. "Do you remember when you first met Jim? You had dated a number of guys when we were in college, but they never lasted. We laughed about your six-week cut. After six weeks or less, you knew it was never going to be a lasting relationship except as friends, and you dumped them. When you met Jim, it was not love at first sight. You two argued about everything, but he made it beyond the six weeks."

"I remember when I first saw the two of you together a good ten years ago," Claire says. "You would get so angry with him when he would say something dumb about women. You let him know exactly what was wrong with that idea. You showed him how strong and intelligent women are, and that he didn't need to protect you from the world. You became partners because you fought for what you believed. You need to do the same with Andrew."

"Go to Sturgis," Denise adds. "Prove to yourself, and to Andrew that you can take care of yourself. You can ride your own bike, and if he wants to see you there, it will be on your own terms. Enjoy yourself, and let him know that is what you are doing."

"It is a long trip, so I'd have to trailer the bike. There will be 350,000 or more people there. I am not likely to just run into him or camp next to him at a campground. I could make the trip there and never see him."

"Do you want to see him? You could call him once you get there. Talk to Sue, she may know if any of the women from her riding group will be there. You talked about the online scooter club. See if someone from it plans to go. If so, you could join a group of scooter riders. I've heard that Sturgis really is for the love of motorcycles."

"Am I really in love with the man? I thought it was just for fun."

"Oh, Maggie, just for fun? Claire and I may have married toads, but that is not your style. Nor are you likely to have a man in every city like Megan. "

"I do not have a man in every city. I may date more than one man at a time, but it is not that easy to have more than two or three. Denise is right. You are in love with Andrew. Show him that you are independent and strong. Tell him when you are angry, but don't throw him away."

"Denise is also right about having married a toad. I'll house and cat-sit for you while you are gone. I'd come with you, but I'll probably need some time off later. I've decided I've wasted too much of my life on my rat of a husband. I discovered that he has a girlfriend once again. This time I'm filing for divorce."

Our conversation quickly moves to Claire and her decision. I guess I need to plan for a trip to the Black Hills. I should also plan to call Andrew before I leave. If I'm going to Sturgis, I at least want to let him know that I'll be there. Maybe I'll ask him to join me for a beer. It will give me a chance to tell him how I expect to be treated as a woman.

Chapter Thirty-Six

I have two weeks to plan my trip. I am a list person. I've yet to make lists of lists, but I do love the old steno pads with an instant two columns for things like "To Do" or "To Pack." The end of the month is always a busy time in mortgage and escrow, but especially so in mid-summer. August will be even worse, so I normally plan my vacation time for late fall or winter. I'll need to wrap things up for all of the July closings and knock out as much of August's preparation work as possible before I leave. Annie can handle the office with backup from a retired escrow agent I've called on for help more than I like to think about these last two years. There are times when I wish I ran a large company with dozens of agents, but on other days I'm happy that it is just the two of us. Annie refused to keep her license active. She says she's happier doing the routine things rather than the responsibility of being a licensed escrow agent. Our system works, so there has never been a need to push it. The office is a simple check off on my to-do list.

Claire has already moved into the guest room. She knows she can stay as long as she wants, but she plans to look for an apartment while I'm gone. I think that she doesn't want to be tempted to go back to her husband once again. She really should have thrown him out of the house. He refused to move, and she didn't want the fight. My heart breaks for her. It makes my issues with Andrew seem so small.

I seriously need to decide what I want to do about the man. I try not to compare Andrew to Jim, but I can't help it. Jim and I seemed to mesh so completely. It wasn't a smooth ride, however. We did struggle with our roles at the same time that I was struggling with my own sense of worth. I remember how often my mother was busy telling me how to keep a man by being a proper lady. She said she got my father because she was so helpless without him. I never felt she was helpless, but my father did buy into that. Jim and I both realized I was never going to be a proper lady when he learned that I swore more than he did. Nor have I ever been helpless. We were equal partners, and I am never going to accept anything less from Andrew. Yelling at him is probably not the best way to explain to him how I expect to be treated. I'll need to have a rational conversation with him. If that doesn't work, I may need to adopt a variation of a younger me plan. Rather than a six-week cut, it will be a six-month cut. I don't even like the sounds of that. I don't want to admit even to myself that my friends are correct. How could I have fallen in love with him?

Mid-week Denise calls to announce that Megan will meet us at Southcenter Mall. They had decided Claire and I both needed new undies to start new chapters in our lives. It was an excuse to get out of the house, and shopping at the Mall could be almost as good as a river walk for exercise. We meet at Victoria Secret. Denise declares that I needed to pack something other than granny panties as part of my riding gear. Megan felt that Claire needed new "play clothes" just in case her life takes a dramatic turn. I am quick to state that I do not wear granny panties, although a thong would not be a good choice for a bike. Claire states that she already owned "play clothes." We just enjoy being together. I surprise myself by finding colors and styles of lingerie that I hadn't considered. I select a few pieces to pack in my suitcase. If Andrew and I do settle our disagreement in Sturgis, I may want to put a smile on his face.

We follow shopping with dinner. The Mall is wrapped in restaurants as well as having the food court, so making a decision can be a challenge. We are creatures of habit and good food. The Mayflower of China is a unanimous choice. We can usually count on Betty, the owner, to join us for at least a few minutes. We've been friends for years, so she likes to hear about any new adventures. Over dinner, I ask for help about how to tell Sharon I've decided to go to Sturgis. Betty suggests that I tell her when I get back. She heads off to greet other diners before we agree that might not be the best plan. Claire says, "I could tell her if she decides to drop by."

"She only lives two blocks away. She drops by all of the time, so it's not like she won't drop in during those two weeks. She is my daughter, so I have to be the one to tell her."

"You could tell her that I was booked to go on a cruise, and the man of the moment dropped out, leaving me with a space to fill," Megan says.

"She knows I don't usually go on vacation at the last minute for the first two weeks in August. August is always a very busy month in the escrow business."

Denise adds, "She would also want to know why you didn't mention the cruise during the party. Just flat out tell her you are going because you want to. She is a big girl. She will get over it. Or she will try to talk you out of it, and then she can deal with her failure. Either way, she will know, and you can go without feeling like you are sneaking away."

"You are right. I am the parent, and it is my decision. I think I've also decided to call Andrew to tell him I'm going to go, and that I do hope to see him there but that I'm not riding with him.

"Good plan. Now have you made reservations at a fancy hotel so you can screw his brains out?"

I have to laugh. "If I'm pulling the trailer for the bike, I'll be in the camper. We should be just fine there if that is what I decide to do. It is also impossible to find a hotel room at such a late date. I'm just glad I've been able to reserve a campsite. Most of them were full, but one right outside of Sturgis just had a cancellation. I hope it won't be too rowdy. The website plays up families with photos of trees and some bikes, but not wall to wall bikes. Other campgrounds advertise their bars and parties. I may want to experience a Sturgis Bike Rally, but I don't want to live a Sturgis wild hog party. I'm also not in a hurry to jump into bed with Andrew again. The sex has been great, but I'm looking for a relationship. I have to deal with the fact that he still manages to say things that just make me crazy."

"Give Andrew a chance to come find you on your terms. It is always good to make a man work for it." Megan states.

The chat with Sharon starts as I had expected. She thinks that I am having a mid-life crisis or trying to recapture my youth through the bike. She actually listens when I explain that my youth was good, and I want this part of my life to be good as well. I decide to declare it good enough when she ends with, "Well, I like Andrew. I think he will be good for you. If he is okay with you riding your bike, I will be as well. I want you to be safe and to have fun. Sturgis is not something I ever want to experience, and I know I won't be telling my friends that you are there. I do love you, Mom."

Calling Andrew is much more of a challenge. It takes me two days of discussions in my head before I can even find the opening words. "Andrew, I wanted to let you know that I will be in Sturgis this next week."

"It doesn't sound like you plan to ride double with me. You are riding your scooter to the rally?"

"Yes and no. I'll trailer my bike to a campground. From there, I can ride anywhere I want to go. I thought we might meet for a beer. I've heard there are lots of places to buy one there."

"My friends like to go to the Full Throttle Saloon. I could meet you there once we all reach the Black Hills. Who knows, you might even accept a ride on my Harley."

"I might. We might also decide to join one of the rides to Devils Tower together. I have learned that a group of scooter riders will be making one of the trips there with members of a Harley club. It might be fun."

"I can't really picture Harleys and scooters going down the road together, but anything could happen. We will be there on Monday. Call me when you arrive. I'll ride over to see you. I've missed you, Maggie. You drive me crazy, but I do like your company."

"I'll call you," making no promise on just when I'll call him.

Chapter Thirty-Seven

The Bergman 650 is not a small scooter. On the drive from Washington to South Dakota, I see a number of RV's with a scooter in a rack on the back of the vehicle. I am driving a camper van, and there is no way the Bergman would fit on a rack. The camper could handle a small 50 cc model in a rack, but not my Bernie. It did take me a while to select a name for the Bergman before Bernie popped into my head. I had wanted a female name, but Bernie, it is. The trailer is designed to hold up to two bikes. It is very easy to ride Bernie onto the trailer and anchor it down. The best part for me is that the trailer is easy to pull and park. The campground manager has assured me there will be room in an extra lot for the trailer once I arrive.

I enjoy the drive. The miles roll by quickly with the ever-changing scenery. I have a number of books on tape to keep me company. I stop when I'm tired and eat when I'm hungry. Being a turtle with my home on my back, I often stop at a rest area for lunch and find campgrounds for the night. I do my research each night and reserve pull-through sites long enough for both the van and the trailer. It is not that I don't like to maneuver the trailer into a small campground site, although that can be an issue. It is just easier to not have to unhook the trailer. I had driven this route with Jim a few years ago, and have marked some good campgrounds on my maps. The GPS also helps me find ones close to the freeway. It isn't that long of a trip. I do not need to push myself.

The trip also gives me a chance to appreciate the beauty of Bernie. At my stop for gas the first day out, a man in a diesel pick-up truck next to me asked about my scooter. He said he rode a dirt bike. I really want to believe he was admiring my bike and not trying to hit on me. At each campground, I have additional people ask about the scooter. A few of them were also heading to Sturgis with their bikes on trailers. Not everyone wants to make the trip on their bike.

The 1,100 miles over three days is giving me time to take it easy. I could get used to traveling by myself. I keep telling myself that with each passing mile. A relaxing trip gives me time to think about riding in the Black Hills with other scooter riders. It also gives me way too much time to think about Andrew. What do I really want from him? I can't see myself just being a bed partner, nor can I picture rushing into a marriage. Do we really have things in common besides the attraction and possibly motorcycles? I've never met his friends or family. I've never seen his office. I don't even know if he is actually a good attorney. I also hear my mother in my head once more. I can hear her voice telling me that a lady never chases after a man. She would never consider driving halfway across the country to ride a motorcycle with thousands of men on motorcycles. Is this really what I want to do, or am I trying to prove something to myself? Do I really want to do this for the right reasons? By the end of the drive, I only know one thing for sure. As much as he drives me nuts, I know I've fallen in love with Andrew. I'm still not sure what steps I should take next, but I'll put him out of my mind and just enjoy riding my bike. Now I need to work hard to turn off my mother's voice once again.

Traffic around Sturgis is heavy and slow. There are motorcycles in every direction. I finally arrive at the campground. There are three motorcyclists ahead of me at check-in. I try not to be impatient. I should have time for a quick ride after I get Bernie offloaded, the trailer unhooked, and the van settled. I want to feel comfortable riding in the heat before calling either Andrew or the scooter group's leader, Beth Ann.

The campground lives up to its promises of trees and a bit of space between sites. After I offload Bernie, I park the trailer in the lot beside a large number of other bike trailers. It appears I'm not the only one to trailer my bike to the rally. When I return to my campsite, I complete my hookups and spread my red and white tablecloth on the picnic table. When Jim and I camped with the children, spreading the tablecloth was a sign that we were actually camping. It is easy to smile at the memory. I really hope I can do all of my traveling here using the bike until it is time to head home again. I am very happy that the site has enough space to park the bike and the van. There is a nice shade tree by the picnic table, and that is surrounded by green grass. As I sit at the table to put on my riding boots, the woman in the RV next to me comes over with her glass of wine in hand. "Hi, I'm Ruthie. Are you getting ready to go for a ride? Are you here by yourself?"

"Ruthie, I'm Maggie, and yes, I'm going for a quick ride before I start cooking dinner for myself."

I have to listen carefully to Ruthie's southern drawl as she happily chatters on nonstop with her free hand highlighting her words. "My husband headed out earlier. He said he'd be back before dark. He likes to meet up with his buddies at one of the bars, but he doesn't usually stay late or drink too much. He just loves coming to Sturgis. I'll go to some of the concerts with him, but I'm not into any of the long rides in the heat or the bars with young girls flashing their tits."

Smiling, I reply. "I'm really concerned about the heat as well, but the forecast is for cooler than normal and a few clouds over the next couple of days. I'm hoping that does not mean rain. I'm not much of a bar woman myself. I would not want to compete with those young ones and their T-shirts."

"I don't like to camp or ride in the rain, but it isn't in the forecast for this week. My children say that traveling in a twenty-eight-foot trailer is not camping. I do point out that the twenty-eight feet includes room for the Harley, but they do have a point. When the kids were small, we camped with a big old heavy, smelly tent. My husband would like to have us ride the Harley and camp with a small tent. I told him no way, so we compromised with the toy hauler."

I laugh, "My late husband and I traded in the tent for a camper van years ago. We had talked about a small tent and the motorcycle, but we never did it. Now it is just me."

"I'm sorry about the loss of your husband. I'm going to fix some spaghetti and a big salad for my dinner. I hate eating alone, so if you'd like to join me, you are welcome. Go for a ride, and I'll have dinner and wine ready in a couple of hours or so. You can tell me all about why you are here by yourself. Does that work for you?"

"Well, thank you. That sounds like fun."

"Who knows, by the time you return, I might find another biker wife or two to join us. Ride safe, and I'll see you later."

As I ride out, I can see that the tenting area of the campground is also full of bikes parked beside each tent. This campground advertises itself as family camping and does not offer the beer garden that is featured at so many other campgrounds. They do have a restaurant that I'm sure is popular with the tenters. I decide to continue up Highway 79 towards Bear Butte State Park for my ride. Google Maps had shown it to be a three and a half-mile ride from the campground. Downtown Sturgis is only five miles away, but I'm not ready to head into that traffic this afternoon.

I had been to Bear Butte once before. When I was twelve, we made a driving/camping trip to the Black Hills. My father was driving that day, and my mother read the map. She announced that we would camp at Bare Butt State

Park that night. My father stopped for gas and asked for directions to Bare Butt.

The service station attendant had a very frosty tone as he was quick to inform him, "Sir, here we call that Bear BUTTE, not Bare Butt!" My father tried hard not to laugh as he thanked the man and got back into the car. He started laughing so hard he had tears in his eyes as he told my mother how embarrassed he was by her mispronunciation. She told him she thought he knew she had been joking. They were quite a pair.

My brother was quick to jump in with, "You mean you were 'In Bare Assed' Dad?" It was a family joke for decades, and over forty years later still makes me smile at the silliness. I am happy that I don't need to ask for directions!

It feels good to settle into the ride. There are lots of other bikers on the road in both directions. The group of Harleys ahead of me are riding two abreast at five miles an hour below the speed limit. There are about ten bikes in the group. There are another fifteen or so about three-quarters of a mile behind me. I wonder if I have gotten in the middle of an official group ride, but the two groups turn off in opposite directions at the next intersection while I continue straight. I do feel accepted when every member of an oncoming group gives me the motorcycle greeting signal of a left hand out low. It is not to be confused with a turn signal given with the wrong hand. I'm happy to note that Andrew is wrong about having my scooter accepted here. Of course, none of those bikers would realize I was riding a scooter until we were even, but I'll think positive. I also stand out because I'm wearing my red helmet, and they just had on do-rags. South Dakota may not require a helmet, but I'm still a safety girl.

After a quick loop through the park and a stop to view the bison at a distance, I head back to the campground. Having Ruthie fix dinner makes my life just a

161 Red Helmet On A Motorcycle

little easier. Two other biker wives join us. Ruthie is the first to ask about my scooter. "So, after your husband died, you bought a scooter so you could ride by yourself? That would take more courage than I have."

"I did. I realized that actually learning to ride at my age was not going to be easy. The automatic transmission on the scooter simplified it just enough."

Chris, another of the biker wives, asked, "Is riding a scooter a good way to meet men? I'm not planning to get rid of my husband any time soon, but I'm wondering if that might be a good option for my daughter."

Mary, the fourth member of the group, said, "Well, coming to Sturgis, worked too well for my teenage daughter. She was only seventeen last year and met an unemployed biker who was here. Took us forever for us to break that up! We left her home with her grandmother this year."

We continued our discussion about the range of bikers and the difficulties of raising daughters until I declared I had to go to bed. Our chat around the campfire with another glass of wine has been a nice way to spend the evening. I did take time to call the organizer for the online scooter group on riding plans for tomorrow. I'm not yet ready to call Andrew. I might need to prove to myself that scooters are accepted at Sturgis before I deal with him. My bed feels a little empty as I crawl in. Will I soon be sharing it with Andrew?

Chapter Thirty-Eight

At 9 AM the next morning, I join the scooter group in the parking lot outside the Full Throttle Saloon off of Highway 34 on the eastern edge of Sturgis. The Full Throttle is a landmark bar and claims to be the world's largest biker bar. Beth Ann, the organizer for the online scooter group, told me last night that at 9 AM, it would still be quiet there, and that it is very easy to find. We will ride from Sturgis to Deadwood, where we will have lunch and time to wander through the sights there before we return by midafternoon. Most of the music venues start in the evening, so we will all be able to go in different directions once we return. I'll admit I'm a bit nervous about the whole thing.

Twenty-five or so women with large scooters makes for an impressive sight. It takes me a couple of minutes to locate Beth Ann. She had told me to look for her ten-gallon hat. It does make a statement. She is surrounded by four or five women in riding gear as she checks each of them on her clipboard. She greets me with a smile as I give her my name. "Maggie from Washington, welcome. Introduce yourself to the others. We only have a few more women who plan to join us."

"How many scooter riders are here in Sturgis?"

"Oh, I would imagine there are a few more who haven't heard about us, but we should have about thirty for the ride this morning."

"Wow, Beth Ann, I thought the ones who are already here make an impressive group."

Beth Ann looks serious, "Thirty out of 350,000 is not a very big percentage. Most of the women at Sturgis ride on the back of someone's Harley. I'm hoping we can show them that women can ride and that scooters can be serious bikes."

She has a point, but I'm still impressed. I also realize that this matches the argument I've had with Andrew. I turn to look at the group of scooter riders. The women are a mixture of ages from mid-twenties to other silver-haired ladies eligible for the Red Helmet Club. The scooters are also a mixture. There are other Bergman 650s and 400s, Honda Silverwings, and Reflexs, as well as BMW and some European and Korean brands I remember from my own bike shopping.

I walk over to a small cluster of other silver-haired riders in time to hear one introduce herself as Sally, and that she has ridden her Silverwing from California. "It was no big deal because I ride over a hundred miles a day to and from work. My riding club makes a two-fifty to three hundred mile trip at least once a month on the weekends."

Another says, "I rode down from North Dakota, but it really isn't that far. I can't imagine riding a hundred miles to and from work. My friends and I have ridden a hundred and fifty miles for weekend shopping trips. Taking the bikes means we eat more than we shop." That is an easy statement to identify with.

Again, I am impressed. This shows the potential, but I have to add, "I really am a lightweight when it comes to riding long distances. I trailered my bike."

"So did I," said a pretty redhead. "I came here years ago with my now ex-husband. I wanted to come back just for me, but there was no way I was riding my BMW from upper New York state."

Beth Ann calls out. "Everyone is now checked in. Ladies, let's get ready to mount up." We all move to our bikes. Sally is parked beside mine. She has a motorcycle GPS system plugged in on her Silverwing. She explains that it was handy on the cross-country trip but is essential for traffic information during her commute. I hadn't thought about GPS for my bike. Traffic in the Puget Sound area can be nasty, so this is something I'll need to consider. For now, it might be a distraction rather than a help until I'm a lot more experienced. I look around at the women. All of the ladies have full helmets and protective riding gear. There wasn't a leather thong visible in the entire group. When Beth calls out the Blue Tooth channel, every woman makes the adjustments before putting on her helmet. We will not need to use the backup hand signals unless someone has a problem. This is a group of serious riders. I'm so glad I had added the Blue Tooth set to my own helmet. I am also surprised at the number of red helmets. Maybe we have our own chapter of the Red Hat society right here on scooters in Sturgis.

The day has dawned warm, but not yet hot. Having vents in my helmet and the mesh in my jacket will help keep me cool on the return trip. It is less than fifteen miles from Sturgis to Deadwood but could take a couple of hours with the traffic through both towns. The group has decided to make the loop north on Highway 34 and then turn south on Highway 85. The return trip will be a more direct route on Alt 14. Like all group rides, we will travel at five miles below the posted speed limit for safety.

As soon as we start to pull out of the parking lot, we are passed by a small group of Harleys. Each of their bikes probably makes twice the noise as our entire group of scooters, and they are going much faster than the speed limit. That fact is not missed by the scooter riders. The radio discussion turns almost nasty until Beth Ann reminds the group that some of the Harley riders could be on the same channel. One of the younger women says, "I'm sorry that I started that rant. I thought my ex-boyfriend was one of the men who passed us." Her tone implies it was not a nice breakup. Others are quick to offer condolences before we settle into comments about the countryside. The rolling hills and valleys of the Black Hills provide a very scenic backdrop for riding. The mountains do not match the Cascades in Washington State, but they are fun to ride. Our scooters are nimble enough to take the inclines and curves with ease. I am pleased that we rode Highway 34 rather than taking Interstate 90, which follows the same route.

As we ride through first the northern edge of Sturgis and then through the city of Whitewood, I am still surprised at the number of bikes everywhere. The 350,000 bikes are spread across all of the towns in the area rather than just in Sturgis. A number of the women are in agreement that rather than the Sturgis Motorcycle Rally renaming it, the Black Hills Rally would be more appropriate. As we near Deadwood, Beth Ann interrupts the light chatter to give directions. We will have lunch at Kevin Costner's Diamond Lil's Bar & Grill. She has made reservations for the group so we will have an area for parking and no waiting for lunch. One of the other silver-haired women asks if Beth Ann also reserved Costner for the group's entertainment. Her response of "Sadly No" was joined by "in your dreams" and even a "but he is so old." We may all ride large scooters as a group, but we clearly have a generation gap.

We park our bikes in a cluster with the others on the west side of the parking lot. The parking attendant has followed the same pattern as the downtown area, a block away from where bikes are lining the west side of the main streets leaving only the east side of the street for car parking. Another group of motorcycles has followed us into the lot and are directed to a nearby open spot. A few of the men stop to look at our bikes, and we hear the familiar question, "What are those things?" We are happy to show off our scooters as well as admire their Harleys. Andrew was correct in saying that most of the bikes at the Rally are Harleys, but so far, no one has said anything derogatory about our scooters.

The restaurant is filled with Costner's movie memorabilia. Unfortunately, the man himself is not present, but lunch is still fun. After lunch, our group splits up as we look at bikes and shop for souvenirs. Beth Ann and I decide to look at the motorcycles lining the main street. By nightfall, the numbers will increase as will the activity in the bars and casinos. The bikes, like the riders, are of all ages and styles. In between Harleys are BMW's and Kawasaki's. We haven't seen any crotch rockets, but Beth Ann says they are there as well. I feel a little like Dorothy in the Wizard of Oz. Rather than lions and tigers and bears, Oh my, it is choppers and ape hangers and Road Kings, Oh my. I realize that Beth Ann is accurate. The variety and number of large scooters pale in comparison to the Harleys. I find myself thinking about Andrew and his Road King. I wonder where he is and what he is doing. It may be time to give him a call.

When my children were younger, they accused me of being a witch, because I seemed to know what they were going to do before they did it. They might have a point, when I spot Andrew standing beside his bike just a few feet away. He gives me his very special smile as we approach. I introduce Beth Ann. She gives us a quick wave as she moves on after reminding me what time we need to be back at our bikes for the return ride. I wonder if knowing a Harley rider is against the rules, but she is planning the combined ride to Devils Tower for the next day, so she must know one or two.

"So you really came, and you are riding, so you brought your scooter. You are also talking to me, so I guess I'm out of the dog house."

"Barely out of the dog house. I'm not a foolish young girl who needs you to make decisions for me, Andrew. We really must learn to discuss things without having one of us blow up and treat the discussion as a threat. We have each done that, but there has to be a better way."

"I will admit I am accustomed to getting my own way. I understand that you need to have an equal standing. You are a strong woman who knows her own mind." Andrew looks down at his boots for a few seconds and then turns those beautiful eyes on me. "Maggie, I think I'm in love with you. You drive me crazy, and we will probably still have rather heated discussions, but I don't want to lose you because I've been stupid."

His words have taken my breath away. *He thinks he is in love with me! Do I tell him that I'm in love with him, too? Is it too soon*? I decide to take a safe route. "Where do we go from here?"

"Well, I'd vote for a hotel room fast, but I doubt if there is one available. Where are you staying? What are your plans for the rest of the week? Do you have tickets for any of the music festivals?"

I can't help but smile. The thought of a hotel room had also crossed my mind. "Well, I decided to go whole hog. I have tickets for Alice Cooper at the Buffalo Chips tonight. I never even listened to him when I was younger, but it sounded like fun. I have the camper van at Creekside campground out near Bear Butte State Park. Tomorrow is the Harley and scooter ride to Devil's Tower. Would you like to join me for either of those?"

Andrew responds, laughing, "I also have tickets for Alice Cooper for the same reason. Do you think Beth Ann will let me join the ride tomorrow if I promise to never say anything against riding a scooter again?"

"She might with that promise. So what are your plans before Alice starts tonight?"

"What if I ride back with you? I'd really like to have some face-to-face time with you, but camping in tents with the guys might not offer any privacy. Think your van might accommodate us?"

"I think I can arrange that. It might be something to consider when we come next year. If I ride with you, we'd probably need to book hotel rooms. Or we can bring both bikes on the trailer with the camper. It would be your choice."

"My choice? At some point, I do want to have you wrap your arms around me on the back of my bike, but you also look good on your own. We have time to discuss it, Maggie. We have lots of time to discuss it."

"Sounds like fun." With that, I put my heart into the kiss I give him in front of all of those motorcycles and motorcycle riders. There is something to be said for the fearlessness of a red helmet on a motorcycle.

About Alyne Bailey

I majored in biology, minored in chemistry and mathematics at a small college in Minnesota in the 60s, which meant that I was the only female science major in the Science Hall. I proceeded to work in many different jobs that were dominated by men. I went back to school at age 55 to receive my Masters in Computer Information Management Systems where I was still one of the few women. I also learned to ride a motorcycle at that same time. I like to think that all of those men helped me become a stronger woman.

When I taught business and computer classes at a small college in Washington state, I offered my students some advice:

"For the first day on a new job, wear your best navy blue suit like the one I'm wearing today. If you have just moved into a new home, however, and can't find your best shoes, follow Jenny Joseph's advice. Wear a red hat with purple that does not match or as I have done, wear your red sneakers and make a statement." I wore my red sneakers with a navy blue suit to start and end each school year.

"Life is too short to wear plain white socks, so go for something fun."

"Set some long long-range goals."
A. One of my long-range goals is to write the Great American novel. Now that I am retired, my husband and I have moved to Texas. With our house restoration completed, I have finally found time to write. That Great American novel is still a work in progress, but this first novel puts me on my way.
B. My second long-range goal is to become a stand-up comedian. My students were to be my practice audience.

Being a stand-up comedian is yet to be explored, but who knows what the future may bring.

Social Media

Facebook: https://www.facebook.com/alyne.bailey.5

Twitter: https://twitter.com/AlyneBailey

Website: https://alynebailey.com/

Acknowledgements

Special thanks to Professor Emeritus Nancy Howard for her patience as she read and reread my revisions so many times. She reminded me where all of those commas needed to go as well as pointing out when I wandered into the past. How could I have forgotten so many rules in the ~~54~~ fifty-four years since my last English comp class?

Thank you to my friends who inspired so many conversations in my head. You are permitted to remain anonymous.

Thank you Jenny Joseph for writing the wonderful poem "Warning!" that has provided inspiration to women of a certain age.

Thank you to the Red Hat Society ™ for making the red hat a badge of honor.

Thank you to Destination Harley™, Fife and Silverdale, Washington for allowing me to add a touch of reality.

Made in the USA
Monee, IL
21 July 2021